Mukul Kumar is a civil servant belonging to the 1997 batch. An Indian Railway Traffic officer, he is presently working in the Ministry of Railways, New Delhi. He has studied humanities from Delhi University. His anthology of English poems titled *The Irrepressible Echoes* was published in 2012. *As Boys Become Men* marks his debut as a novelist.

You can contact the author at info@mukulkumar.co.in or follow him on Twitter @writermukul

Praise for the book

Mihir recalls the past, right from his first day in college where he runs into ragging to that moment of elation when he finds he is finally in. And between the two points, there is a great deal—friendship, hard work, career choices, responsibility to family and their expectations, first love, the rhythms of life in a metropolis, regional differences and prejudice, and much more. And keep an eye out for three major motifs—Mona Lisa, Soma and Shiva—and the spirited discussions on history, religion, sociology, philosophy, psychology (especially that of love and sex)—and even Bollywood. ...the author uses the frame of preparing for and getting into civil services to present an engaging picture of experience in any career, once the initial gloss has dried.

—*The Times of India*

MUKUL KUMAR

Published by
Rupa Publications India Pvt. Ltd 2016
7/16, Ansari Road, Daryaganj
New Delhi 110002

Sales centres:
Allahabad Bengaluru Chennai
Hyderabad Jaipur Kathmandu
Kolkata Mumbai

ISBN: 978-81-291-3852-1

Second impression 2016

10 9 8 7 6 5 4 3 2

Dedicated to Shiva, my saviour

Contents

Capsule of Present

'These days, I feel completely deflated, unable to carry on living. I feel like there is nothing to nudge me forward; nothing in my future calling to me,' Mihir starts sulking, having thrown himself onto the sofa with a thud conveying the hollowness within.

Mihir has just returned from work. 'Oh! The same usual outbursts; I am getting sick and tired. What happened? Did the Minister's PA dodge you again on his assurance of getting you a house out of the Minister's quota?' Ruchi asks, her face showing a mix of scorn and empathy. She sits opposite Mihir in the living room after asking the maid to make some tea and snacks.

'The issue is not the government accommodation; and you know what I mean, but you deliberately guide the discussion towards practical issues to avoid my whining,' Mihir says with contempt. But deep within, in such moments he cannot miss the positive side of the firm realism in Ruchi's approach; if not life, at least living has to move on.

'That is because I know your outbursts don't make any sense and don't lead anywhere. I have never heard you talking about ways to fix your problems. What you talk of is completely impractical. "I want to get away from this job. If I could have my destiny pull me out and put me on a course to happiness! And blah, blah, blah...!" For God's sake, please start talking reason,' Ruchi's tone changes to one of fury. Mihir's repeated bouts of melancholy have become alarmingly frequent after getting transferred to Delhi from Shivpur.

'But what do I do? Job, house—nothing seems to arouse my interest at all!' Mihir continues whining.

'Please stop this now and tell me what was the outcome of your meeting with the Minister's PA?' Ruchi comes back to the point while handing Mihir a cup of tea, her tone echoing a firm resolve to arrest Mihir's drift into his illusory world.

'Yes, I met him and he assured again that it would take some time but would get done for sure,' Mihir replies with a conscious effort to infuse some optimism into his words to avoid blowing out the faint spark of hope on Ruchi's face.

Mihir is constantly fighting his dejections. He remembers how, when they were leaving Shivpur's sprawling bungalow for Delhi, he had told Ruchi with a sense of animated pride that he had succeeded in eliciting the assurance of the Minister's khaas PA, impressing upon him the urgent need of the house for his old parents. The Minister belonged to the region of Shivpur and Mihir had facilitated many things for his constituency during the four glorious years of his stint there.

'But I am not sure whether his "some time" will ever be a time!' Smiling sarcastically, Mihir does not forget to blend the optimism with caution.

Ruchi while smiling at Mihir's sarcasm says, 'But that is how things happen. You have to keep meeting him till you get something in hand and you have to go the Delhi way. You can't expect him to deliver in the first go and you must appreciate how many like you harangue him for such favours. They too may be in dire need like you. After all a Cabinet Minister is not a joke!'

'But I extended my full cooperation to...'

'What you claim to have done, I am sure, would never beat official protocol. You are not the kind to go out of the way to accommodate anybody, so put aside the thought of any privilege on that account. It can't be treated as a quid pro quo,' Ruchi interrupts, smug at showing him reality.

The idea that his efforts do not immediately entitle him to a house under the Minister's quota has already begun sinking in. But he is frustrated that Ruchi, as usual, is deliberately avoiding the bigger picture he wants her to see.

'Hear me out patiently without getting irritated or interrupting me,' Mihir is ready to let out his pent-up emotions. 'You have seen how many times we had to go on pilgrimage to school to prostrate in front of the Principal; that is what Ravikant and many already in Delhi had indoctrinated into me for conquering the school for Geet. Besides, I couldn't get into any worthwhile assignment despite having a fit profile. But you are witnessing what is happening—I am just whiling away my time here. It is a world where the realization of your worth depends upon others and a change in the viewer changes your worth.'

Ruchi doesn't pay much heed. 'It has always been like that and you are just feeling it more because you are having to taste it in fuller measure here. You grumbled about these things earlier as well, if you remember. But you could manage these feelings earlier as there were other things to balance them out. Mr Kumar, for God's sake, please realize that bureaucracy is inherently impersonal; individual sensitivities don't matter. Yet you keep looking for it. Why do you make yourself miserable this way?'

'Oh God! How powerless this makes me feel and how frightening to seek worth without? But yes I confess that the sense of deflation had started since the last days of Shivpur,' Mihir poured out in almost a single breath.

'Not just the last few days but almost throughout. I can still remember you saying, "I am tired of being here. There is a lot of pressure and this is too high a mental cost for buying importance. I am convinced that I am not meant for it and my calling is different..." And so on and so forth,' Ruchi reminds him, painting Mihir again in the colour she has chosen for him.

It is almost dinner time. After having their tea, they remain in the sitting room. The next day being Saturday, they know they can afford this luxury of an extended evening without tomorrow intruding into it.

Ruchi tells Mihir to change and come back for dinner. She sits in the dining room while Mihir walks into the bedroom, asking Geet about her school and studies. When Mihir returns and sits at the table he thinks, 'This house, the sitting room, the bedroom, the dining table—this luxury of a defined living is a borrowed affair.'

The house they are living in has been arranged by one of Mihir's friends, Gautam. The house was owned by Gautam's partner and was supposed to undergo renovation but he deferred it by a few months. Gautam has given Mihir this luxury till he succeeds in getting a government house. That is what at least Gautam hopes.

At the table Mihir and Ruchi pick up the conversation from where they had left it in the sitting room. Mihir begins, 'You very well know where my calling lies.'

'You wish to write full-time. I know it is your passion, your dream, but what's the point of just constantly harping on it?' Ruchi asks, mellowing out a little bit as she touches on something Mihir likes.

'Yes!' The mere mention of writing makes Mihir happy. He has finally steered the conversation towards where he wanted.

'But why can't you appreciate that your job and your writing can't be mutually exclusive, even though you wish them to be. Come down to reality and understand that the kitchen fire must be kept burning. I don't earn, remember?' Ruchi counters the happiness Mihir feels.

'This is where my hopelessness comes from. You may accuse me of indulging in wishful thinking but you must appreciate that leave alone quitting, I can't even opt for a sabbatical because I know the discomfort my displacement will get you all into. That too here in Delhi at this stage when we are not getting tired of feeling miserable. My dear! I care for you all more in deeds than words,' Mihir says, projecting himself as a responsible family man.

'Yes! Here lies the contradiction in your personality, which I can neither appreciate nor understand. You sulk just for the sake of sulking; you have figured out your passion but don't try to find a path to it. This is nothing less than tragic. You never sound genuinely concerned about resolving the conflict between your passion and your profession, finding a way to reconcile your writing with your job,' Ruchi says while shushing Mihir as he begins to speak. She continues, 'I accept that it is easier said than done, but let us also accept that what is tough will remain tough no matter how much we whine. It's high time you try to fit your writing into the present scheme of things. There is no other way. Fortunately where you are now you are getting extra time that you can devote to your writing, but you waste all of it sulking about your professional worth and other things.' Ruchi sounds empathetic and agitated all at once.

Dinner is proving to be a completely mechanical affair, a sort of a ritual; hot chapattis on their plates are getting cold as they are too engrossed in talking to eat.

'I accept that my being within bureaucracy breeds ambition and you know that is also my hunger. I either want to be completely out of the world of my job, rid of ambition, so that I can pursue my passion, or I want to remain completely within at a position which affords me my worth. You may call me hypersensitive but I am what I am,' Mihir retorts.

But deep within Mihir realizes that his thinking serves no practical purpose. Reality will not change the way he wants it to and Ruchi makes sense. A student of psychology, she has a natural flair for words of wisdom. Mihir often thinks when he is arguing with Ruchi that accomplishments and practical wisdom need not necessarily converge.

Ruchi immediately replies, 'There again you are contradicting yourself; you claim you are a family man. Given that, our present is going to remain the same. So why can you not write at the same time?'

'And what about me seeking professional worth?' Mihir asks,

pointing out the flaw in Ruchi's argument.

'At Shivpur you had this worth in full measure but you still abandoned that and decided to come to Delhi due to "a sensitive post, monotony and emotional discomfort". This kind of sensibility is contrarian to the world of bureaucracy. See, in Delhi, things will remain the same till you succeed in changing your assignment, which is not certain. Secondly, even if you succeed, you may get your professional worth but not your writing. So, my dear, where does your writing figure? You are thoroughly confused about what you ultimately want—your ambition or your passion. Like many you are betraying your passion for your profession. There is no world beyond a job, family comforts intact, where you get to live out your dream. And don't start again, "Alas! If our ancestral riches were not squandered by my grandfather..." Those complaints will not revive the riches to afford you the luxury of quitting your job and taking to writing full-time. Nor does it seem feasible that you will find an important and challenging post that affords you the time for your writing; that is just wishful thinking. I am surprised that I have to be telling all this to someone who thinks deeply! It's high time you get your priorities right, for your sake and for ours as well.'

'So?' Mihir asks irritably.

'So you need to wed your job and your writing for your own happiness because you can't have only one thing in your life. Now I am tired of counselling you,' Ruchi replies impatiently.

On hearing Ruchi's words the Mona Lisa springs to Mihir's mind, sparks of hope brightening up his despair.

For him, Mona Lisa defines an indecipherable emotion or situation in life, where pleasure and pain are both mixed. Just as it is a mystery whether Mona Lisa's smile is happy or sad, so too are certain points in life where one can only say one is painted in the Mona Lisa hue.

'What do I do? This writing doesn't leave me alone even if I want to get rid of it. Free from it, even if I am discontent with my situation, at least I am at peace with myself. Otherwise I am constantly at war with myself, divided into two beings. I always find another self travelling with me, assessing, appraising, analysing and approving my actions, thoughts, feelings, emotions, perceptions and my entire being. A parallel self that only torments me.'

'You are divided between your profession and passion, and this parallel self you are talking about is actually your writing self, which is rising because of it being unfulfilled. So start writing and your two selves will merge to give you a sense of fulfillment and happiness,' Ruchi counsels assertively.

'But I can only handle one thing at a time, my job or the writing. I can't manage the spillover of my profession into my passion, spoiling the placidity of my mind,' Mihir justifies himself.

'Oh, your mind is impossible. Then don't curse your destiny if you can't get into action,' Ruchi relents.

'Madam, that is again easier said than done. The battle of mind is not that easy to win,' Mihir replies, at once going against both himself and Ruchi.

Ruchi, asks the maid to clear the table and continues, 'What I intend to drive into your brain is that life rarely falls into order as per your commands; you have to strike order out of chaos. Mr Kumar, pursuing your passion entails huge mental strength and it is not easy. The earlier this fact sinks in the better it is for you.'

Ruchi thinks, 'He claims that his favourite muse is *life* itself, yet why can't he understand this?'

Mihir slides into a pensive mood, Ruchi's reason finally mellowing his irreconcilable rigidities.

'Come on! Let's go out for some jalebis. Won't that be wonderful? The hot sugary syrup sapping some chill out of our bodies on this cold day,' Ruchi proposes.

Geet instantly seconds, 'Yes, Mamma! Jalebis and winter go together wonderfully; we can take Meeta didi too (the help who is more like an elder sister to her).'

They all set out, Mihir and Ruchi with a joyous Geet and Meeta forming two duos walking in tandem to Green Park market, which is known for its roadside stalls that churn out hot and crispy jalebis.

Again Mihir and Ruchi pick up from where they had left off. Tonight appears to be the sort of night they seriously put together their heads to attain some order out of the mess life often throws at them. Post-dinner strolls have always been like laboratories to them, giving them the place to invent ways to bring order out of chaos.

Mihir begins, 'Alas! If it were within my power to conquer myself! It is not like I have not tried. I would be fulfilling a dream if I could seek power within instead of without and this is something only my writing can give me. This compulsive obsession with telling the world a story is tormenting me into a restless creature and my office domain continues to spill into my passions. You are right that my urge to attain single-mindedness is in vain and that my wish to tell a story must not get bogged down by the weight of living. I know I have to stop ruing "my lack of freedom under a regimen", "my drudgery", "my lack of challenges in life" and "my maladjustment to Delhi". I have to let my job be my foundation so that it can prop up my writing and not hold it back.'

'Thank God! Finally I can see some better sense prevailing upon you. I only hope it sustains and doesn't fizzle out like it has many times before,' Ruchi replies. She can't help but think, 'It will be nothing less than a miracle if something conclusive springs up tonight to shape up our lives.'

'Even I hope this time reason and the realities of life prevail upon me and my rational self doesn't get defeated,' Mihir says doubtfully.

'You have to muster your will power. Everyone finds it difficult to conquer their minds, but that is what the pursuit of passion demands; you have to fight this out. So, my dear, leave this Mihir in the living and set the other Mihir, your writing self, out to write a story to get happiness and life into your living,' Ruchi explains simply.

'You make sense. But writing isn't as easy as just taking a plunge and getting started. I have no training in the field.'

'There you go again. You finally are arriving at pursuing your passion and then you begin doubting your abilities,' Ruchi says exasperatedly but is encouraged to continue after seeing Mihir's expression.

They arrive at the shop and order jalebis. Mihir can sense Ruchi's desperation to help Mihir as well as herself. She seems visibly sick of Mihir's sulking and it is something that has affected even her mental harmony. She can show positivity even during the seemingly darkest recesses of life and is now pleading with Mihir to hear her out calmly.

She continues, 'Coming to your fears of a lack of training, I strongly disagree. You are out to make the same mistakes you have made before. You still regret your bad preparations for your civil services exams. How you tended to get scatterbrained, wasting your time discovering the ideal method of preparation; you didn't believe in yourself and kept looking for some formula that could help you. It is something you keep preaching even to Geet. The fact that you realized much later that everything you needed was inside you. All you needed was focus and concentration.'

Mihir is still not free from his doubts and he counters, 'But what about the contemplation to conceive a palatable story. For that you need a calm, centred, orderly mind, but...'

Ruchi is at her unrelenting best, fuelled by the prospect that Mihir is finally mellowing out. Eating the luscious jalebis, with Geet and Meeta engaged in a gleeful exchange of their own, she continues, 'But where is it prescribed that one must be trained to write a story? Why can't you write the story of a man living in his world? As a storyteller, you undertake the journey into the thoughts and consciousness of Mihir. You communicate to the world, a world he carries, I mean communicate "you in-situ". Every man's life is a story in itself representing myriad themes like pain, pleasure, happiness, grief, success, failure, desire, dejection, ambition, trials, tribulations, love, hatred, everything. In fact every life is a drama starring many characters including your kith and kin, friends and foes, anybody you meet. While the realities of life are more or less the same, the characters and contexts vary from individual to individual. Who better than you to appreciate this as someone who revels in writing verses on life itself!'

Mihir is listening to Ruchi, amazed at the depth hidden behind the sheen of a seemingly happy-go-lucky self and realizes that appearances truly are deceptive.

Ruchi resumes, 'Coming to your problem of not having a kick, I find you more often than not revisiting your past and turning nostalgic, fondly remembering the days when you had some challenging goal in your life. You are a creature who relishes the past, so why not wed your past with your writing? Write about your exciting journey to your cherished destination; the trials, the tribulations, the frustrations, the acts of commission and omission, the ecstasy of arriving at your cherished destination i.e., civil services. Write about how you kept shutting all the doors opening for you before you achieved your final destination. That would be an exciting tale of a man chasing his ambition, pushing himself to the cliff of "either there or nowhere". That would truly be a reliving of your past and will give you an exciting vehicle to tread the path to reach your dream destination of becoming a writer. That is nothing short of a double bonanza!

'Then comes the next part of the story. The story of how the cherished destination of civil services changed into a trap. A government servant in his professional context, bored with monotony, enslaved to a regimen without any sense of freedom, and demotivated by not being able to give his best. Write about what you could give to the system and what the system gave back to you—your sensitivities, vulnerabilities, miseries; your solace and ecstasies.'

'Okay. Let me try resisting my natural inclination to becoming depressed. I will try channelling my depression into my writing,' Mihir assures her as a promise.

Enjoying the thrill out of her success in arranging the Rubik's Cube of Mihir's mind, Ruchi says, 'Let me tell you this Mihir, your context is ideal to afford you the time to write. Don't allow this steam to escape the fissures of your mind with your sulking and whining. Look within yourself and I know you will find everything falling into a coherent whole, and a story could emerge on its own, for yourself, for many other Mihirs, and for the world.'

Mihir looks at Ruchi hypnotized, thinking, 'Words can be so powerful that I can tame the monster my own mind has created!'

'Mind you, this challenge will be bigger, and the kick will be sublime. When you wrote your examinations, you just had to study with single-minded focus, with your parents supporting you, but now the odds are huge and you have to resist the pressures of your job spilling over into your writing mind. You have to steal your writing time, resisting even your family intruding into your writing. Mr Kumar, believe me, the battle to conquer your mind will be both thrilling and satisfying,' Ruchi says.

The family gets home and prepares for bed. His head hitting the pillow, his eyes shut, Mihir is instantly transported into his mind. Mihir's mind and melancholia usually go together; but tonight he ushers into his mind not despair but hope. Though his mind still remains tumultuous, Mihir sees ecstasy rising from his heart gradually dispelling his pessimism. His mind has unravelled into an inspiring order; the present, the past, the sense of challenge, his family, his writing, all fall into a resonating symphony, a lullaby. This happens without any material change in life. It is magical. That is when Mihir decides to write from within his present life.

Mihir's writing self has been set free and it begins a journey through a dream. His writing self pronounces, 'I hope this journey proves to be an exciting one and fulfils this dream.'

~

Entry into Past

Looking back, life is breaking up into a few snapshots and vignettes. I don't know why only these particular ones are coming to the fore. They have probably sustained and survived the rigours of time because they are intense. The mind has a unique mechanism of retaining the intense events of one's life; events that evoke strong emotions. These lie embedded deep in the unconscious, subconscious and sometimes in the conscious as well. I believe these must be the ones which have impressed upon my sensibilities to produce the being I am and the world I have lived in—the content, the contours and the context. Standing here I only have these snapshots and vignettes at my disposal to dig out my past to write a story. I hope these will prove to be the capsules which when pieced together with my conscious, will flow into the expanse of time gone by to emerge through words.

But standing at the gateway to my past, I feel engulfed by the riotous rush of my emotions, apparently too convoluted to be configured into a coherent whole. The truth of being and the reality of the life I have lived; why I thought what I thought; whether my thoughts and emotions were right or wrong; whether 'right' or 'wrong' is absolute or relative; whether reality is also many-sided; whether truth is achievable or not; whether 'truth' is only a chimera, and the process of living is the only profound truth, instead of the sublime entity we call truth. All of this is just confusing.

Emotions are overtaking my expressions and I feel trapped between the two. But at the same time I firmly believe that a story is also trapped inside, screaming to emerge. So I will not get bogged down and I will tell the story, resisting the temptation to judge, leaving the rest to my readers, hoping that this story of an individual is capable of depicting the universal, Ruchi's 'slice of the whole'.

The story now.

Where do I begin? In his present life Mihir is missing a challenging goal, so let me catch him right during his pursuit of a challenging goal, his cherished destination—the civil services.

~

Baptism into CS

'Nawab sahab! Please take the trouble to look at us also. After all, we too are your subjects,' a boy calls to Mihir loudly.

Mihir turns to look at him, unsure whether the call is for him. It is one of the three boys sitting on the inner fence along the drive-in in front of the college.

'Yes! Of course! We are pleading before you,' the boy says, settling Mihir's doubts. He has a mischievous smile with an unambiguous hue of villiany. Chewing his gum, he intermittently grits his teeth to convey a bossy swagger. He looks too grown up for college and could safely be called a giant. He is intimidating, tall and broad, his muscular body visible beneath his tight T-shirt. He has a dusky complexion, a biggish face and thick features; with two protruding teeth providing a sort of black and white contrast, accentuating his villainous aura.

Mihir stops, his shy and submissive gait projecting a meek, 'Yes?'

'Janaab! We are not such commoners as to not even deserve an introduction. It seems like you are a fresher. Please come over; you are welcome,' the boy calls to Mihir again, his words definitely not matching his expression which is sort of sarcasm soaked into villainy.

Mihir keeps standing where he is, by now completely aware of their intent. They are pestering him with their gesticulating hands; smelling danger, Mihir ambles towards them.

'What is your name?'

'Mihir,' he says meekly.

'You walk like a Nawab.' They hint at Mihir's reserved gait. 'So you must like music. It is the eternal passion of the Nawabs, isn't it? Do you also sing?'

'No.' Mihir positions himself away from them, conveying his desperation to get away.

'Do you listen to music? We don't think you can disagree; everybody listens to some music,' the boy says.

Mihir is getting acutely anxious.

'Who is your favourite singer?' the boy asks before Mihir can reply to the previous question.

Mihir keeps mum, his posture conveying utter shyness.

'Not answering will not save you.' The boy gets bossier.

'Kishore Kumar,' Mihir just manages to be audible.

'Which song?'

Mihir keeps mum again, hoping that his response thus far and his pusillanimous posture may win him liberation.

'Sorry we can't hear your answer,' they mock Mihir's nervous mumbling.

'*Tere chehre mein woh jaadu hai,*' Mihir answers in a meek voice.

'Oh wow, am I that attractive? Even if I am, I hope everything is okay with this Nawab. He may afford to have a "different" liking but hats off to his courage for disclosing it with such élan! Has this assumed such free expression in our country?' the boy grins, looking at the person sitting next to him.

Mihir now knows he is in deep trouble. He starts looking around helplessly, praying for some intervention, but nobody comes to his rescue. The guys and girls around him just glance at him and walk away.

'We just don't want this to be artificial. We are all natural and want the song to be targeted at the right audience,' the boy grins demonically.

Mihir is gripped with a feverish nervousness, his mind alternating between 'Run away' and 'But these boys will catch me anyway.'

'Okay. Let us lend this helpless creature some help. Nawab sahab, why don't you look around for the right audience for this song?' the boy says without a hint of sarcasm.

Mihir feigns ignorance, hoping against hope for a miracle.

'Can't you look for some "chehra with jaadu" around? I never knew that such a severe drought has hit Kirori Mal College. If he can't, let us pick one for him. Okay look, there are three girls standing just near the gate. Can you see the tallest one of the lot wearing an all-white churidar? I think she is the most beautiful face here. Now go to her and sing the first two lines of the song,' the boy says as his friends laugh monstrously.

Mihir is terrified and he can only feel his heart beating loudly. He wishes in vain for the earth to swallow him or even better, to swallow the villain right in front of him.

'Hey man! Enough is enough. You have taken long enough.

Now we have to take care of the other preys too. Go,' the boy says with a tone of finality.

Mihir inches towards the girls, feeling as if his two limbs are heavy as logs; by now he is a miserable heap.

'Man! Move faster!'

Mihir thinks, 'Only the ugly like him can be this villainous.' He continues to walk slowly, the consequences of disobedience uppermost in his mind. Then the image of a naked boy being paraded around college strikes his mind, and he thinks for a second that that might be a lesser evil.

'Hurry up!' The command comes again.

He finds himself only a few yards away from the tall girl. Mihir surreptitiously looks at her. In his mind, 'I should do. I should not do, I can do, I cannot do, what if I don't do?' plays like a broken record. He weighs the naked parade against a resounding slap from the girl. Given his king-size ego when it comes to girls, the latter might be the worse punishment. He knows his good looks and reserved demeanour prop up his ego. He has never followed girls. It is the other way around.

Mihir is fidgeting with fear, inviting the attention of the girl. She glances at him; and as he keeps standing there, the glance turns into a stare. The stare then becomes ferocious, her face turning stern. Mihir continues to stand there, the boys deriving sadistic pleasure from his discomfort. He mulls over telling the girl the truth but knows this may land him in deeper trouble.

'Can I help you?' the girl asks sternly.

'*Tere chehre mein woh jaadu hai*… Sorry but I have to do it,' he sputters and before the girl can react, Mihir sprints away, passing by the boys and going as far as he can before crashing into a lanky boy. That helps the throbbing pace in Mihir's body settle down, and his heart slowly returns to normal. Mihir doesn't say anything; he is still too nervous.

'Is it those boys? I am Sandeep, a fresher like you,' the lanky boy says, pointing at the villains who are still grinning sadistically.

'Yes! It was a bit too much,' a panting Mihir manages to convey his horror between gasps. He is still scared that the girl will come after him. Sandeep cools him down by saying, 'We will take care of it, don't worry. I think even the girl probably understands that this is a part of ragging. Let's go to the canteen and grab a cup of coffee.'

Today, Mihir is remembering this fleeting flashback of his first day in college as he walks down the fateful drive-in to collect his degree after his graduation. He ruminates fondly how 'the tall girl', Jyoti, kept conveying to Mihir her inclinations through different means—soft fleeting glances, long gazes, frozen stares, piercing smiles, inviting frowns, inventive confrontations, deliberate disappearances—and also how he and Sandeep became friends.

'Hi! Going to collect your degree?' Sandeep sees Mihir and stops him.

Mihir thinks, 'Today again the spell has been broken by Sandeep!' Chemistry and coincidence are beyond logic and tend to transcend into the realm of surreal.

'Yes! How do you feel holding your degree and finally walking out into the real world?' Mihir asks, pretty sure Sandeep would respond with nostalgia.

'Ha! Three years seem to have gone by in a wink. Will you ever be able to forget those animated discussions before classes that we used to have right here in this corridor and all those singing sessions we never wanted to end,' Sandeep replies, taking Mihir's bait.

'And me constantly pestering you for a Kishore Kumar number, pulling you out of your Rafi spell. I always thought you sang Kishore better,' Mihir responds, his urgency for his degree fading.

'No way! There is no one to beat Rafi; his voice and his classical depth are matchless. Actually you are just infatuated with Kishore Kumar,' Sandeep says.

'Infatuated? No way! It was always me who would talk reason. There is no "why" to music; if you like it, you like it. There is no explanation as to why a particular voice gives you ecstasy. You can never explain it and for me that magic voice was Kishore's,' Mihir responds.

'But then you must appreciate that singing Rafi's songs is always tougher.' Sandeep doesn't let go.

'Ah! Again theorizing. Let me give you proof. When you sang, I could always sense more ears invited to a Kishore number,' Mihir replies, frustrated at Sandeep missing the obvious.

In no time, it seemed like another day in college, when Sandeep and Mihir would passionately sing Rafi versus Kishore songs between their classes. It was just one of the many things that the two used to have passionate arguments about.

'Forget your Kishore, what about Jyoti? That exchange of gazes was truly enjoyable and how can we forget that "smooching couple" in the courtyard! They left all of us flustered. I even felt a pang of depravation. It was obvious by how much Jyoti would blush that she liked you, and she never missed an opportunity to look at you then. Dear brother, you can't say you didn't like her as well because your fleeting glances at her said everything, though you thought no one was noticing,' Sandeep says playfully.

Sandeep is enjoying the sight of Mihir's face turning red with embarrassment.

'A bit of that can actually continue even now. She is also enrolling for her post graduation,' Mihir says mischievously, startling Sandeep.

'Bloody hell! You have been following her so discreetly that we couldn't even guess!' Sandeep says joyfully.

'Forget about Jyoti, look who's coming; it's the ever-dandy Suds.' Mihir points towards Sudhir.

Sudhir is of average height and build, with a dusky complexion. His hair is parted in the middle. He wears glasses on his oval face and though he is average-looking, he is clean-shaven and dressed in neat formals. One often finds him unconsciously checking his tucked-in shirt and the parting of his hair, making sure he looks immaculate. His smile accentuates his air of reticence and makes him appear like he is eternally guarding something inside himself.

Sandeep, knowing Sudhir's nature, taunts, 'Come on, man! Just look at the crisp creases of his clothes and the shine on his shoes! Will the day ever come when we can see you slightly dishevelled?'

'Let it go, man! What about the man you are talking to, huh?' Sudhir tries to shift the focus away from himself.

'What do I say about "Mysterious Mihir"? He was born good-looking. He doesn't have to work on his dressing and grooming to look good,' Sandeep says, with a naughty smile, patting Mihir's back.

Mihir is tall with a broad frame. He has a wheatish complexion with sharp features; his eyes are conspicuously black and defined, accentuating his good looks and his bushy hair is parted on the right. His shyness lends him a look of vulnerability. He seems reserved, which is often misunderstood as ego. But there is an unmistakable streak of swagger in him that comes from the attention he knows he commands.

'Mysterious Mihir! What is this new nickname I missed out on?' Sudhir asks.

'Absolutely new! He earned it just now. This gentleman has been following Jyoti without even giving us a hint,' Sandeep replies.

Mihir cleverly diverts the topic, 'Who can forget the squeaking of those shiny shoes that always got louder in the presence of Prof. Sahni, the one man who truly hated that noise and would glare daggers at Suds constantly! But our Suds never paid any attention and kept his cacophony alive.'

Sudhir smiles mischievously and Sandeep says, 'He was nothing less than a crook who pressed his feet harder on the ground whenever he saw Prof. Sahni. Over the last three years he has perfected the art of producing different notes through his squeaks.'

Before the three friends get completely lost in their world of nostalgia, Moti Ram, a senior office clerk, appears and asks, 'Have you collected your degrees? You also have to make sure that you have your no-dues certificates with you.'

'Oh yes! We have to hurry up. They are probably waiting for us to finish,' Mihir pushed Sudhir, who had also not collected his degree.

'Sandeep, if you wait for a bit, we can leave together,' Sudhir says.

Mihir, Sandeep and Sudhir are together in the canteen and have decided to continue their nostalgia trip.

'Let's order some bread pakodas and coffee. I'll just go buy a fag from Tingoo; I saw him around here,' Sandeep proposed.

'Yes! Let me complete the usual order and buy some chewing gum from "Tingoo" of Amitabh Bachchan fame,' Mihir says, revelling in the college association, though indirect, with his favourite actor. Mihir often boasted as if adoring Amitabh Bachchan meant being a bit of Bachchan himself.

Though there were quite a few of Sud's 'luscious lasses' and Sandy's 'campus birds,' in the canteen, today the 'birdwatching' chemistry is just not working out despite Sandeep stealing naughty glances at the girls; it appears more laboured than natural.

'So when are you vacating the hostel?' Mihir asks Sandeep.

'I was supposed to vacate within a week but I'm not sure if I can find a new house by then. It makes sense to start preparing for civil services quickly. I am looking for a place in Mukherjee Nagar (popularly known as MN) since it is the best place for sincere CS (civil services) aspirants,' Sandeep says seriously.

Mukherjee Nagar is arguably the most popular locality in the Delhi University campus. The suburb is a sort of refuge for DU students who don't live in the hostel and even non-DU people who migrate to Delhi for competitive exams.

'Yes it is easier to manage accommodation there. Flats get vacated at the end of academic sessions since the pass-outs and aspirants, "dead" or "alive", usually leave,' Sudhir says smugly, since he has already been living there for the last three years. He couldn't get a room in the hostel nor did he ever try applying for one.

'I'm also trying for a place in MN. Who has the patience to wait for a slot in the PG hostel? A very good friend of mine, Uday, already lives there but he, too, is planning to shift out and he is looking for a serious CS aspirant as a roommate. Uday is graduating in history this year and like us, he too is preparing for CS. We have already been talking about living with each other,' Mihir says, gesturing at the canteen boy to generously add Cadbury drinking chocolate powder on top of his coffee.

'Well said! It is wise to live with like-minded people. By any chance, can I join in? One of my Hatian (the pass-outs of the famous Netarhat school in Bihar) friends has offered to take me in but he is a non-CS guy; plus there's nothing like forming a history gang with you guys,' Sandeep says while blowing smoke rings. He seems sombre at the thought of vacating the hostel, and he looks at the smoke rings as if trying to find the nostalgia escaping through them.

Smokers tend to shape their smoke rings to fit their emotions. Looks-wise, Sandeep fits into the smoker group quite easily. Mihir identifies smokers as people who are 'skeleton thin' and have a 'hazy texture of face'. He always imagines a fag sucking the oxygen from the smoker's body instead of the other way around.

Sandeep is thin and bony, bordering on tall. A small but visible hump on his back gives the impression of an arched posture. He also has a long face that adds to his lanky frame.

'In fact, that would be wonderful. Flats with two bedrooms are easier to find. Suds should know better, though,' Mihir says, drinking his Cadbury-coated coffee, but inwardly he thinks, 'Alas! I wish I were living alone.'

Even though Mihir has friends, he tends to restrict

togetherness, zealously guarding his solitude, especially at night. In bed he never wants anyone around, preferring to be by himself, with his mind, and his heart.

'That's quite right. MN is pretty costly that way and prices are shooting up every year. It's simple economics. Everyone wants to live there. Otherwise not too far away is Indira Vihar which is also manageable. Actually Batra cinema makes MN all the more coveted,' Suds expands on his 'MN expert' status.

'Well, why shouldn't it be coveted? There has to be a premium on ambience and this locality definitely has that. Everyone I have met says it,' Sandeep says, lighting another cigarette, making Mihir uneasy since the smell of tobacco irritates him.

'A premium for Batra!' Mihir steals a naughty glance at Sudhir before casting a mischievous smile at Sandeep. 'Batra means night show movies and "birdwatching" as well, right Suds?'

'Yes! Birds of different feathers with local flavour lent by Punjabi kudis to the pan-Indian breed. By that I mean female students of different states make the mix truly exciting,' Suds says, high on the thought of girls.

Mihir is growing uneasy, knowing that Sud's flavour will turn raunchy if Sandeep starts on 'girls' since his repertoire is not adulterated with any refinement. Mihir, for his age, is a contrast and his interest in girls is not even truly 'social', subdued with refinement and deliberately slid in only to fit in to the group.

Like his solitude, Mihir guards his urges like a hawk, shy about giving away even a covert hint, let alone talking about them overtly. In his company his friends deliberately make things raunchy to elicit an expression of shy humour from him.

The three suddenly realize that it'll soon be evening. The number of people around them has reduced and the noise of utensils being washed heightens the sense of overall emptiness.

'Wow! Looks like we have stayed too long, it's already three o'clock! We should leave,' Mihir says. 'I have to get my no-dues form and also winding up everything else will need some attention.' Mihir is thinking of his hostel room, and also the nostalgia which will hit him when he enters it.

'Hey Mihir, listen. Why don't you drop in at my place in the evening? It's my turn to host the Hatians today and Sandeep will also be there,' Sudhir tells Mihir as they get up to leave.

'That will be great,' Sandeep says to Mihir.

'But it's a Hatian affair, right?'

'That's a non-issue. Many of them know you, so you are coming,' Suds insists.

'But I've already decided to meet Uday. We have to discuss the new flat.'

'That is even better. Bring him along. Then you, Sandy and Uday can figure out the details of living together. Also, just imagine, Kishore Kumar and beer! Sandy has already been training to sing and you also get to meet the senior CS guys,' Sudhir does not relent.

Mihir is just getting used to having alcohol at parties. Beginning with denial and refusal, he is finally coming around to drinking only beer to dilute his sense of guilt.

Mihir thinks about Uday and knows that he can be stubborn and might be hesitant about coming to Sudhir's place without an invite.

'Why are you hesitating? If Uday is like you and he too is the kind of person who needs to be specially invited to such get-togethers, then I'll come to his flat and drag both of you along,' Sudhir says.

Mihir is now fully convinced of Sudhir's wish for his presence and realizes that he wants to make the best out of the time and effort he has invested into organizing the evening.

'Okay, I'll try my best. I only hope Uday has not planned anything else.'

The three are standing at the back gate of Kirori Mal College, also called KMC, Mihir and Sudhir are heading to the hostel while Sudhir is headed to Kamla Nagar market aka KN—the favourite haunt of DU students.

'Thank God we have not changed our college and remain enrolled with KMC for our MA. We will get to visit KN every now and then.' Sudhir has apparently turned a bit nostalgic mentioning it to Mihir and Sandeep as they walk towards the exit.

'Nothing beats KN as a hangout zone.'

Besides Bachchan, KN is another eternal source of pride for the KMC lot. The line goes, 'All rivulets flowing into this river of joy flow through KMC.'

Mihir has taken a bus from Patel Chest to MN. Since the bus is not too full, he gets a window seat and retreats into his favourite refuge—his mind. He finds himself doing this pretty often since his life has begun changing. Today nostalgia is adding to his usual melancholy and he thinks, 'I have graduated from this life and I am about to enter another world. Out of the comfort of the college regimen, I'm now moving on an uncertain voyage towards my cherished destination, which appears both exciting and frightening at once. What if there? What if not there?'

The bus stops and he walks to Uday's place, not just seeing but absorbing the sights of the place that will now become his new world.

'Hey! You will live a hundred years. I was just thinking about you,' Uday looked a bit off colour.

'Well, it has been a long day. I collected my degree, cleared the library dues, and delved into a nostalgia trip with some college friends in the KMC canteen—Sudhir, whom I think you know because we met him at Batra once, and Sandeep, who is very much like you. Sandeep was talking to me about shifting with us because he also wants the company of CS aspirants,' Mihir says, sitting on the chair Uday has offered. Mihir guides the conversation to Sudhir so that he can pop the invitation into the picture.

'Oh yes, you call him Suds, right? The boy with the constipated smile, who is sort of finicky about his glasses, if I recall correctly. Sandeep I haven't met.'

'You are right about Sudhir,' Mihir says.

'Even I collected my certificate today and was affected by the thought of leaving. There is nothing that can beat the fun of college. How about gorging on some mutton? My Bahadur is already cooking it.'

'That's wonderful. We can eat it tomorrow; you know how good day-old mutton tastes.'

'Tomorrow? Why? What about dinner then? Do you have some other plans?' Uday shoots a flurry of questions at Mihir.

Mihir is gauging Uday's face, hoping he won't get into one of his stubborn moods. 'Actually Suds, I mean Sudhir, wants both of us to visit his place. He is hosting a Hatians get-together.'

'How are we part of Hatians?'

'He still wants us there. He threatened to drag us from your place if we didn't show up. Come along, it will be fun,' Mihir says, hoisting Uday up.

'Okay then. Let me get ready.'

'Quickly please,' Mihir knows Uday takes time to get dressed.

Uday changes his clothes, walking around the room without any inhibitions because his roommate has gone out.

'You'll floor everyone there with this combination,' Mihir says admiringly. He never misses complimenting him because he knows Uday will return the favour.

'Look at you! You're killing in that shirt and boot-cut jeans flaring down on your suede sandals,' Uday retorts playfully.

'What about your slim-fit shirt tucked tightly into perfectly fitted jeans? This combination of sky blue and white looks really good on you!' Mihir doesn't want to be left behind in showering compliments. 'Now all you need to do is to wear your ankle boots for a look that girls would die for!'

This is a normal conversation between Mihir and Uday, both good-looking in their own distinct ways. While Mihir is sober and graceful, Uday is confidently flamboyant, but both have a sense of swagger. At such times Uday would often say, 'Leos are Leos; the king always attracts.' Both Mihir and Uday's sun sign is Leo and, with nobody else to compete with, they carry the tag with élan.

Uday is of average height but has a broad frame. He's muscular thanks to his gym sessions and is extraordinarily fair. He has sharp features on a roundish face and wears his hair brushed back without any parting. He wears glasses which lend his face a mellowing influence, consciously dresses up smartly to accentuate the aura of a stud and never forgets to roll his sleeves up to exhibit his biceps. Though conscious of not being tall, he makes up for it with his gait—chest out, shoulders firm with his hands angled away from his sides to accentuate the swagger of his body.

Mihir and Uday head to Sudhir's.

'Have you thought about Sandeep living with us?' Mihir asks.

'I don't think there is any issue. You know he is a good guy and I trust your judgement. Also, places with two bedrooms are easier to find and it makes perfect sense economically,' Uday agrees to live with Sandeep.

Mihir and Uday grow a bit conscious as some girls pass by. They test the attention they receive out of the corners of their eyes.

'Mihir, did you notice how she was ogling at you?'

'No way! I saw her looking at you!'

'That proves you were watching her!' Uday embarrasses him.

Absorbed in the friendly duel, Uday and Mihir reach Sudhir's house.

'There seems to be quite a crowd already,' Mihir says apprehensively, wearing an awkward expression, as always unsure of getting noticed. He immediately starts looking for someone he knows. Mihir is normally more at ease in smaller groups.

'Let us go inside and look for Suds. We'll probably run into others we know too,' Uday walks in confidently with Mihir, instantly dispelling the unease with his flamboyance.

'Hey Mihir, I was just looking for you. Sandeep is around somewhere, maybe at the back, chatting. Go ahead and find him and I will follow you,' Sudhir says like a good host.

Mihir introduces Uday, 'Meet Uday.'

'Hello. It's good to meet you. Please make yourself comfortable; we'll have a great time today,' Sudhir says.

'These over-the-counter guides are a big no-no, keep away from them.'

Mihir and Uday hear a voice emanating from the middle of a group inside the inner courtyard of the flat.

The courtyard opens through a door into the rear lane, separating two rows of the houses in the colony. Basically there are two entries and exits to each house and the rear exit of the two opposite houses face each other. The boys living in the inner rooms tend to use the back doors to avoid disturbing the inhabitants of the front room.

Mihir stands on his toes and tries to spot Sandeep in the group. The group inside comprises a bunch of guys who are huddled together, listening in rapt attention to a relatively senior-looking guy, his glasses enhancing the seniority of his looks.

'There he is. Hey Sandeep!' Mihir says quietly, shoving his way in to gently pluck him out, conscious of not spoiling the tempo of the group.

'When did you hit the market? Is this Uday?' Sandeep asks.

'Yes, it is him,' Mihir introduces Uday to Sandeep. 'Before we lose ourselves in this party, I want to let you know that the three of us will be living together.' Mihir smiles.

'That's great news! It's a big worry off my head,' Sandeep says happily.

Uday and Sandeep come to strike an instant chemistry. In hardly a few minutes they become friends, animatedly chatting with each other, as if they have known each other forever.

'Okay then, come along. This here is Rajiv Verma. He cleared his mains this year and will now be appearing for the CS interview, most probably in the first week of June. We are asking him for some useful tips,' Sandeep pulls Mihir and Uday into the group. By then Sudhir is also back, nudging the three forward.

Sudhir looks smug in making Mihir and Uday meet a potential civil servant.

'These guides are just cut-paste stuff,' Rajiv Verma is still sermonizing. 'Just don't be tempted to skip the original books, right from NCERTs to the biblical Bipan Chandra, Mahajan, A.L. Basham and Romila Thapar. That is the real slog.' He was talking about the history portion of the preparation, knowing fully well the history gang gathered in front of him.

'But Sir, what is the harm if we find everything in one place? Isn't that a lot of labour saved? I've seen a Reddy's guide book that appears to cover everything. I have learnt that the pactice lessons cover the contents of all the major books you were just mentioning,' a boy asks. He seems like someone who has been recently baptized into the preparations, more intent on eliciting a response than refuting Rajiv Sir.

'But then it misses out the critical topics. Don't make this sort of mistake. While you are going through your preparation for prelims, don't forget to keep an eye on mains as well. That is where these ready-made guides don't help,' Rajiv Verma says authoritatively, still preening on his 'cleared mains' status.

The CS spirit is already flowing. The sound of clinking bottles and the smell of chilled beer fills the air. The excitement is both audible as well as visible.

'Guys! Enough of this CS talk. That will always be there.

Let's have some fun this evening. We are getting some beer and I hope Sandy and Gaurav are ready for some long sessions of Kishore Kumar renditions,' Sudhir says excitedly. While the crowd is helping themselves to beer, CS is still being discussed sporadically. Two young entrants are glued to Rajiv 'Sir', their devotion suggesting that mere proximity will fulfil their hopes.

'Sir, did you never even touch the guides?' the boys ask in a hushed tone.

'Who said that? There are 2–3 questions in prelims this year that were asked from 7th standard NCERT textbooks; at times these guides help in answering such questions, but the mains warrant thoroughness.' Sir continues to soak in the godly status he has been given.

'Sir, how do you go about General Studies?'

'Simple. Everything under the sun. How a Keralite dances, how Spiderman plays rugby, the types of tribals who look the same, the size of the Pygmies, the habitat of the Eskimos, the President of some country you may not know exists, some alien which has recently hit the space. Everything. It's so simple it screws you over.' The air around Sir turns sombre, stifling the bonhomie of the evening.

Mihir and Uday are standing nearby, prompting Sandeep to sing as well as he can. Overhearing Rajiv, Mihir thinks, 'I was told 80–85 out of 120 questions in History is a safe bet. In that case what is the point of going crazy with accessing all the stuff?' Despite Mihir's consciously cultivated reticence, Uday knows what he is thinking.

'What happened? Feeling torn even before the grind has begun? My cousin was right. He said this preparation screws you from all possible angles, virtually tearing through you,'

Uday says, with a barely audible 'enjoy-the-inevitable-slaughter' laughter.

'Spare them now. Why are you scaring them? They know what they have gotten themselves into,' Sudhir says. 'Guys! Get your beers and prepare for some music. Sandy is taking off!' Sandy gulps a little beer to moisten his throat. Meanwhile two Bahadurs, one hired for the occasion, are navigating the available spaces with fried chicken. 'Hush, here he goes!' Sudhir screams, duly supported by his gesticulating flatmate, Rajan. Sandeep is holding a writing board as a makeshift tabla and two juniors are holding steel glasses with spoons for rhythm. He begins, '*Dekha na haye re, socha na haye re, rakh di nishane pe jaan.*' Everyone applauds instantly as the song echoes in the air. All the boys are exhilarated as the song aptly describes their plunge into CS. A few beers down, the euphoria turns resonant, orchestrating an enchanting spell. The combination of CS and beer is buoying everyone's spirits. 'Whatever the result there is nothing to beat the IAS (Indian Administrative Services). The pursuit of these three magical letters gives one a high,' a tipsy Suds says to Mihir and Uday on his way to the kitchen.

Like the CS, Mihir and Uday have been newly baptized into the world of alcohol. If you are an infant in this world, scared of getting tipsy, you tend to judge your kick at each sip and this hyper-consciousness keeps the actual kick controlled. When you think you have arrived at 'toddler tipsy', your target, you have actually ended up having had more than you thought; and when you are off your mind, the actual high kicks in, dropping you at the 'adult tipsy'. That is the mistake Uday and Mihir have made and whenever they have tried drinking in the past, they have ended up feeling miserable. For Mihir the 'Kishore euphoria' lends a multiplier effect, tossing him into a sort of a trance.

'Are you also feeling a mix of pain and pleasure? Leaving college is generating a Mona Lisa kind of emotion. This bloody nostalgia always dodges definitions. College days are gone with all their fun, ushering one into this fuck we call CS. You have invited this fuck for yourself; it's painful, no, pleasurable, no, painfully pleasurable I think—again a Mona Lisa here! Bloody God only knows what it is but it is bloody addictive!' Mihir is dangerously high, and is holding Uday's shoulders. He is slurring, his sentences dwindling off and on into unconsciousness, but he is still trying to gather himself and retrieve the lost words to make some sense.

'Don't worry, Mihir. We will deal with this fuck you call CS. We will take this great wild bull by its horns. But yes, college life is college life! Even I feel cast out into a ruthless world,' says Uday on a high, his loud, booming stupor befitting his flamboyance. Sandeep, still singing, is pausing only to guzzle down the beer; and Sudhir also seems visibly drunk. The atmosphere is enchanting, painted with different hues of emotions; and the confluence of CS, nostalgia, Kishore and beer is mesmerizing.

So the party continues with everyone swinging and swaying. Music, beer, chicken, animated conversations, jokes and laughter, and fun and frolic in the face of the solid CS fuck looming large.

Mihir, Uday and Sandeep are now in the inner courtyard. Someone nudges Sandeep.

'Hey guys, this is Dheeraj. He lives close by and is pursuing Company Secretary course after his B.Com.'

Dheeraj whispers to Mihir and Uday, 'Last year my Sameer Sir, stifled in the tangle of this bloody CS, committed suicide by consuming a full bottle of rat poison. He had appeared in the interview thrice; a brilliant student who was seen as a sure shot. I am telling you, this fucking thing is very dangerous.'

Mihir thinks, 'This boy is probably justifying his not pursuing CS this way because he feels like the odd man out.'

Mihir's thoughts about Dheeraj are interrupted by a commotion of cheers erupting from the front room.

'Aha! Big brother!' scream many at once. Sudhir barges into the room and the others also go in to see what is happening.

'What a solid surprise! How come you are here, now that you are a big man?' Sudhir is excited.

'Actually, we are on a Bharat Darshan with Delhi as the first stopover after Mussorie. I have just come to our MN out of nostalgia! How can I ever forget this place?'

'That's great!' Those who know the new person are already flocking towards him.

'It's a perfect day to be here. You can meet everyone you know in one place,' Sudhir escorts him to a chair vacated just for him.

'The credit goes to Bahadur. I was lighting a fag at Chaddha stores. He met me there and now here I am.'

By now his identity is known to all. He is Vivek Singh, IAS, who used to live in MN. Sudhir and his roommate, Rajan are showing Vivek off to their friends as the 'big man'.

Mihir, as is his wont, notices Dheeraj, who he knows is feeling out of place, and thinks, 'In this phantasmagorical world that he is witnessing right now, CS is the supreme God of the religion of ambition. Anybody pursuing a different career worships a lesser God and is held in contempt. Come to this place only if you are capable of the rigours the worship of the supreme God demands.' Mihir wonders if he is decided and determined about his goal.

Mihir, Uday and Sandeep leave the party, having finally called it a night. They are still high and sloshed in bonhomie.

'Tonight was fabulous and I'm dying to get to my hostel bed. It was a bit too much!' Sandeep stutters.

'We should take the night special from the MN bus stand. That way we can drop Uday closer to his place,' Mihir tells Sandeep, pulling Uday in a side hug.

'Sure! Alas, if we could only fly to the hostel,' a lazy Sandeep says.

'But I feel like flying high in the sky. This is a miracle only beer can induce! They say only God can perform miracles, but I have never seen them. Wait! I have seen it once when suddenly my father disappeared when I was a child; God's vanishing act! Maybe his miracles only bring pain,' Uday releases himself from Mihir's grip and starts running down the road, his hands spread out like wings, with a sense of unbridled liberation. Suddenly he stops by the side of the road to take a leak and Mihir and Sandeep watch him. 'Beer turns people into pissing machines but there is nothing like pissing out in the open, standing on top of a mountain. No no, it's like standing in the heavens! That too at this hour of the night when no one is around! It gives an unmatchable sense of liberation. Apparently pissing in the open is being banned. They make laws only to take away liberation.' Uday's booming voice fills the air.

'Yes! It's a spring getting released from the mountain in a free fall motion,' Mihir says. 'That is probably how the Gods scaled the heights to the heavens—by guzzling soma rasa, the heavenly drink! Whoever makes such a law would also be enjoying benefits of pissing in the open. Dine out, piss out! This is a temptation no one can resist, not even lawmakers who, in their impersonal wisdom, prescribe walking berserk with a bloated bladder in a state of not knowing the world. I feel claustrophobic going into the dingy public toilets that they want us to use. Then what option is left if everything is captivated by a bloated bladder? You either die of bloating or relieve yourself with a thrilling sense of liberation,' Mihir too is stuttering. It is a long rendition; soma somehow lends him a long tongue. Mihir wonders, 'Denied permission, would I give up pissing on the streets?' and then relieves himself like Uday before the confusion deepens.

Sandeep, who has lit a cigarette, starts pissing while smoking; and says, 'But Mihir! Was Vedic soma alcoholic? I think they are still researching on that.'

'No Sandy, not again and not now! Debating even when you are high!. See it's simple; I can't say whether soma rasa was alcoholic or not but I am sure the Gods drank alcohol. No one can fly high without alcohol and since they drank only soma, it has to be alcoholic. I am calling them alcohol drinkers because eternally high on soma, they got stuck in the heavens, beyond death,' Mihir says, rising to the challenge.

'You are right. Our beer isn't as potent as soma, which is why we fall short of heaven and are left to die on earth. But imagine life without beer—not even the momentary highs. Just horrific!' Sandeep expands on Mihir's logic.

'You guys are still falling short of absolute logic. While soma has no side effects and is a beneficial drink, beer does have side effects. The Gods, and the rishis who were their favourites, took advantage of being the first in the cosmos to mop out the best, leaving the inferior stuff for man so that he wouldn't attain immortality and fly to the heavens. If it was us, we would've done it too. Whoever comes first and gets the best consumes it all, leaving nothing or perhaps only the inferior stuff for the rest,' Uday preaches.

'And why have you two missed out Lord Soma, the beneficent plant, the giver of the intoxicating elixir? Let me tell you, the Moon God being called Lord Soma is not a coincidence. He was the cup the other Gods drank the soma from; just see how intoxicated with smugness he is, shining high in the sky,' Sandeep says.

'Now when both Somas are no longer powerful enough to manufacture and serve soma, man has stopped worshipping them. In fact, angry at not getting soma, man conquered one Soma, the Moon God, by stamping his feet upon Him. Otherwise can we even think of touching God with our feet? And the other soma, the elixir plant, is invisible.' Mihir's melancholy assumes a metaphysical hue.

'What do you mean? Does God exist at man's will or is it man who makes God serve him?' Uday is angry with God.

'Can't you see, man hunts for all the Gods; he believes in God only till he has not hunted Him out. He haunts eternity for being eternal; flying in his spaceships to quash the Gods and discover the mystery of soma.' Mihir is soaring high into philosophy.

'Enough is enough! No more wasting time on an unseen God. I'm worried about my world. Let's get real. I have heard they want to ban smoking in public places. As if an urge is a switch that can be turned on and off. Smoke is the younger brother of soma. Lord Shiva always supplemented his soma with grass. The law is a cap on liberation.' Sandeep changes the subject, and adds, 'And lawmakers are also pissing from a height. Earlier they were high on power and now they are addicted to heights! I often think how thrilling it would be for a cop to piss in the open without being afraid of the law! It would be a double bonanza; liberation from the bladder coupled with liberation from the law.'

'You're right. They are mistaking the law for mind control. So because they are finding it difficult to teach control, they are inventing laws that fuck with freedom,' Mihir says analytically.

Euphoria has a penchant for centring on a muse. The muse for this night is soma and pissing.

The three disperse at the MN stand with a bus scheduled to arrive shortly.

'Goodnight, guys! Sorry, I meant good pissing night! A litre of beer down and we are pissing machines tonight. We'll meet tomorrow,' Uday heads home while Mihir and Sandeep heave themselves somehow to get into the bus. Mihir's mind is still captivated by the fleeting snapshots of the CS spirit.

~

Mihir's Tryst with CS—A Few Snapshots

Back from Sudhir's, Mihir's consciousness lasts only till he flings himself on his hostel bed. The fleeting snapshots of the time at Sudhir's, though, are still in his mind and are now amplified. The nostalgia coming from a gradually emptying room had already been giving him a heavy heart and tonight it's like fodder waiting for the fire as he lies on the bed. The realm of the mind is reigned over by chaos; it is rare that it throws up some cogent logic and any claim to its logic being absolute is like claiming to have seen God. Mihir, an incorrigible inhabitant of the realm of the mind, desperate for rationality, slides into the dangerous depth where the rarely found coherence dissolves back into a nebulous haze.

But tonight that rarity is taking place. The logic for his fixation with the CS is being illuminated by the revelatory flashes in his mind, with some snapshots in particular coming to the fore.

Snapshot I

Sitagarh, a small mofussil town in Bihar. Identities fly thick and fast here; to be somebody is not a very difficult proposition that demands gigantic endeavours. If you are distinctive in your field you can hit the peak immediately.

M.C. College is the best in the town. Mihir's father is a teacher in the college, so the association with the college itself affords some distinction. Add to that his being rated the best teacher in the department and the distinctiveness of his identity is anybody's guess.

This teacher has an intonation and expression capable of carrying the delectable symphony of the English language. Besides, his personality is imbued with a keen sense of literature thanks to his being privileged enough to interact with some luminaries in the field during his studies. Thus, he emerges as the numero uno in his department. The consciousness of this distinction has woven an aura around him. He commands respect and awe all at once. His pride is intense and palpable. His evening excursions are inundated with reverent virtual and verbal prostrations by everyone who meets him. His humble acknowledgement of these suggests a proud acceptance.

A young boy, innocent and considered intelligent, always first in class, who idolizes his father with a sense of pride.

It is the school's annual day. On stage, a young Mihir is being lauded by the Principal with a stash of prizes in his hands stacking almost up to his chin. The Principal announces, 'As usual this boy has earned the first position in almost all academic events, be it the exams or debating.' Looking at his father in the front row, he continues, 'And why not ? Like father, like son.

Let me take this opportunity to request his parents to leave him free and unfettered to aim for the civil services.'

Snapshot II

It is a congregation of Mihir's father's family members at Faizpur in Uttar Pradesh where Mihir's grandparents live. The group includes the grandparents, the four uncles and one aunt, Mihir's father, and their families. This is something that is meant to celebrate the togetherness of three generations but invariably ends up as an epitaph to the lost grandeur and riches the family, one of the famous Taluqdars of Avadh, once commanded.

'An aeon has passed but it remains baffling how such huge fortunes could vanish, how Babuji (Mihir's grandfather) could go on a destruction spree without any regard for his children's well-being,' Mihir's father says, his face and posture displaying complete amazement; his eyebrows raised, creating furrows on his forehead; his mouth open; his lower arm lifted from the elbow with his hand frozen in the air.

'Yes, every grain and inch,' affirms Majhle Papa (Mihir's eldest uncle). 'Even Amma's (mother's) jewellery, if spared, would have been sufficient to raise us.'

'Oh Bhaiya! Why get into this again? We never tire of talking about this. Shouldn't we be indebted to God for blessing us with an elder brother like Bade Bhaiya (Mihir's father) who devoted himself to nurturing us?' Mihir's Buaji (aunt) chips in.

'He was our saviour and we are what we are today because of him. It is as simple as that,' Majhle Papa says.

'It is all God's grace and man is merely the means,' Mihir's father says humbly.

'There is no denying that but don't you all feel that we could rescue ourselves out of the sea of insecurity and ignominy only because our circumstances made us desperate and determined?' Chhote Papa (Mihir's youngest uncle) says.

The focus shifts to Chhote Papa and his glorious success in the civil services.

'Well, what can we say?' Buaji replies. 'He salvaged some of the family's pride and pulled us out of ignominy by competing in the civil services.'

'He was a brilliant chap right through. His teacher vouched for his making it into the services one day,' Mihir's father says.

Majhle Papa continues, 'It was certainly a feat imbued with a sense of prestige and aura associated with the family of Raja Sahib (Mihir's grandfather). Bade Bhaiya would also have made it but for the circumstances that bogged him down. He had to take care of us and I guess that is how destiny willed it.' Being immediately younger to his Bade Bhaiya, he remembered his brother's compulsions and tribulations vividly and had a better appreciation of the sacrifices that had been made.

'Bygones are bygones. Let's not talk about me anymore. I never got to ponder over ambition and aspirations. These terms were redundant in my context,' Mihir's father says sombrely.

Mihir starts thinking, 'The civil services are the ultimate consummation of academic excellence. My father, though a teacher of huge reputation at Sitagarh, still nurses the pangs of not being able to pursue a career in the civil services. The Indian Civil Services are said to befit Raja Sahib's aura and that means they are kingly in form.' Chhote Papa's schoolteachers vouching for his being part of the services gives Mihir a sense of déjà vu.

'Only listening to your uncle's achievements will not lead you all anywhere. You all now have access to the means to pursue your studies. Why don't any of you at least start dreaming of repeating his feat?' Mihir's grandmother's words bring him back to reality.

Snapshot III

Mihir is in Sitagarh, Bihar, at a Kendriya Vidyalaya. The school is abuzz with commotion and simmering with hushed murmuring, suggestive of caution and concern. Though the classes are on as usual there is an uneasy stir in the school's rhythm. The school wears a more orderly, tidier look; the signage, flowerpots and furniture are all where they should be. The teachers and staff are running around because it is the day for the inspection of the school by the District Magistrate, the ex-officio Chairman.

After a while, a man is seen walking the corridors, surrounded by teachers and staff; his swagger conveying a sense of authority. The Principal, whom the students treat with awe and respect, is also subservient despite his apparent seniority. Mihir is filled with unease, watching his normally dignified Principal bowing.

'Such a young man gets the oldies quaking in their own school. Had I been in their place, he wouldn't be repeating his visit,' the words of a student leak out, reaching the teacher in the class.

'My dear friends! He is the DM! He is the Zille ka Maalik, understood?' Jha Sir says.

Hearing the words Zille ka Maalik, Ganesh, one of the students in the class, stands up. Popularly known as Gutsy Ganesh, being too hefty and tall for his class, the boy has an intimidating gait. His shoulders and neck are perpetually thrust forward, his hands separated from his sides in a firm flare, his elbows protruded to accentuate the haughtiness. Somehow no class is complete without these few samples who have grown beyond their age, giving the teachers a run for their respect.

Ganesh asks, 'Sir, just in our last class our civics teacher, Gajbiye Sir, taught us that the DM is a public servant whose basic function is to ensure that the people in his district live in peace so as to maintain law and order. He is responsible for ensuring that the people in the district get the due benefits of the government schemes for education, food, infrastructure etc. How come a public servant commands so much awe and authority that our masters are treating him like their master? To me this sounds antithetical.'

The teacher, not in the mood to encourage him, replies, 'You shouldn't be curious about these things. Studies and you are antithetical, you won't understand. At least let the classes run properly so that others get to study and can aspire to become DMs.'

Mihir thinks, 'As a public servant one can make a huge difference to the lives of the people. Over and above that a public servant is accorded so much respect, awe and authority by the society. Service and authority combined will be a heady cocktail.'

Snapshot IV

A young Mihir succeeds in getting into the engineering stream in college. Train reservations have been made for his departure. A day before his departure, Mihir says to his mother, 'Ma, I strongly feel that engineering is not my cup of tea. An engineering degree may tempt me into the world of jobs and would make me complacent towards civil service preparations.'

His mother counsels, 'These days even engineers are writing the civil services exam successfully. To me it sounds like a much better proposition.'

'But this backup may weaken my determination to get into the services since for engineers writing CS, their degree is just a backup. If one chooses to be an engineer out of passion why would one write these exams? It is a compulsion, not a choice,' Mihir says.

Suddenly, Mihir sees his father smiling. He has overheard the conversation while sitting in the verandah. He opens the cupboard, takes out the train ticket and tears it into shreds while saying, 'My son will not be forced into anything. He basically doesn't want to study engineering and is interested in humanities. His happiness is my first priority and our happiness ultimately lies in his happiness. I am with you, my boy.'

A huge burden of expectation is immediately cast on Mihir's shoulders and the civil services are engraved in his mind.

~

The Trio Anchors in Mukherjee Nagar

'I am feeling out of it today. I need a change,' Uday sighs.

'But this mess needs more work to bring it to a semblance of order,' Mihir says. He knows Uday's typical restlessness; he can't ever remain still for too long.

Sandeep instantly seconds Uday, smiling mischievously at Mihir. 'I think we must go out for a change this evening. Don't you want to inaugurate Batra? It will feel bad.'

'Yes, Mihir. You are new to MN. There are certain rules for living here and prostration before Batra cinema is a custom. How about doing it when "Bachchan Boss" is on the move again? *Hum* is already a declared blockbuster.'

Sandeep beams at Mihir and says, 'Some greenery will also afford us the chance for birdwatching.'

'Okay, let's go for a night show. We have some time before that. I have to arrange my cupboard and fix my lampshade and I can see you two also have a lot to do.' Mihir goes to his room.

Mihir, Sandeep and Uday have rented a two-room flat. Mihir has insisted on being alone in the smaller of the two rooms to guard his solitude. He is not the messy kind; he craves order. The sight of books, clothes and magazines in chaos offends him. Even as a hosteller, he never compromised on recreating a dimly lit ambience with the help of the lampshades matching his melancholic moods. His mind gets lit up at night.

Some order achieved, the three go to Batra. They have planned to eat out as well.

'We are going to Zen,' declares Uday, suggesting he knows the place.

'Sure, we'll take your word for it,' Sandeep says, already focused on bird watching.

They are heading to the restaurant, if it can be called that, known to serve mouth-watering Punjabi–Chinese hot and spicy food.

Mihir thinks, 'India is a country of remarkable adaptation and assimilation. The weirdest of ingredients make a delicious dish.'

They are passing Batra. It is a huge commercial complex by the main road, with a movie theatre on the ground floor. On the other sides are rows of all kinds of shops, general stores, grocery stores, restaurants, resto bars, liquor shops, juice bars, book shops, printing booths and phone booths.

Right in front of Batra is the DTC bus stand. And separated by a lane is a big magazine stall, an expansive layout displaying career magazines and guides, a place with holy scriptures for the civil services, the supreme God. It has always been a ritual for all to check for new arrivals lest they should miss out on them.

The atmosphere is filled with various activities. This is a miniature economy supported by the pilgrims who have migrated in search of their Gods, a world in itself, charged with aspirations and ambitions. 'Upon these hunters for survival depend the survival of so many!' Mihir thinks.

'I think before settling down to eat we should buy tickets for the movie,' suggests Sandeep.

'It's already a month old. We'll get tickets for sure,' Uday says.

'They serve some fantastic chicken chilli and hakka noodles here,' Uday mentions when they reach the restaurant.

'Sure, let's get those,' Mihir says, looking at Sandeep for approval.

'Okay, no issues,' Sandeep signals to the waiter to take the order.

'Man, this place is electric. I think we will enjoy our stay here,' Mihir says , his eyes sparkling.

'Yes, if at all the screw spares us,' Sandeep says, reminding them of the ensuing slog.

'That will take care of itself, don't worry. Getting into a groove at a new place may take some time,' Mihir says, hinting at them cleaning up.

'Overall the deal was not too bad. The aunty agreed at Rs. 1,200. Even Rs. 1,500 would have been beyond what we could afford,' Uday says smugly. 'Please get us some Coke as well,' he orders.

'But at the start she really scared us with all the, "You people are from Bihar? Let me check with my husband first. Don't feel bad but people don't speak well of Biharis here,"' Sandeep says angrily.

'Here Biharis form the biggest diaspora. Punjabis don't have a choice but to rent out to them. It is a question of making money and not only that, this entire region thrives on the demand of us students. We spend money on rent and dhabas here in Delhi. Otherwise, just think, if we would not come, this money would be making Bihar richer,' Mihir says on the issue, growing sombre.

'Yes, that is right. Don't you remember Aunty herself mentioning that rents are shooting up every year and even her husband's store has seen a boom in sales? We are making them richer. But for Bihar's pathetic education system, we wouldn't be here,' Uday agrees with Mihir.

'In fact, Punjabis and Biharis get along pretty well with each other. For that matter many students from the northeast of the country are also flooding this place. The same paucity of education has pushed them to Delhi. The funda is simple—it's a give-and-take relationship where they trade on our ambition and we trade on the opportunities here. Can we even smell the hangover of the Hindu–Sikh riots that tore this place apart just a few years back?' Sandeep says in his usual way.

'You're right. It isn't for nothing that they say economy is the solution to discrimination. I doubt Mizos and Nagas would be hissing at Delhi with such venom if we allowed them equal access to economic benefits,' Uday joined in.

'Okay. Have you already started studying for CS? Where is this coming from?' Mihir questions Uday playfully.

The food breaks the rhythm of their conversation.

'Drop all this now and look there,' Uday whispers to Sandeep. 'Wow! Just perfectly endowed,' he guides their gaze to a beautiful girl sitting just adjacent to their table.

'There you go again!' Mihir says as he eats.

'Mend your ways a little at least now that you have

graduated. Let the world know that you are not a kid anymore.' Uday smiles at Mihir naughtily. 'Brother, I feel you probably already have someone in your life. I'm sure someone must have fallen for such a handsome man.'

'No no. There is no one for me yet,' Mihir says, shying away from Uday.

'You're right. He is already playing hide-and-seek with a girl from KMC,' Sandeep chimes in. 'Why are you lying? Haven't you told Uday about Jyoti?'

'Okay! You're keeping secrets!' Uday says, happy to have found a way into Mihir's secret world.

'It's nothing of the sort. Sandy, can you even call it an affair?' Mihir says. And then turning to Uday, 'I have not even spoken to her.'

'One thing is for sure. If she has fallen for you, you are also pretty keen on her. Have you forgotten those gazes you both exchanged in college, especially in that corridor?'

'No point making a mountain of a molehill. First tell us about Sanjana,' Mihir turns the focus on Uday, prodding Sandeep to push Uday for more.

'Hey! You also have been keeping secrets!' Sandeep says, readying himself to extract information out of Uday.

'No way. I have no secrets about my urges. She is a Venky girl but it is just a fling. I am not the kind to get involved in senti hanky-panky,' Uday says.

'Mihir, have you met her?' Sandeep asks.

'Yes, once at his place. Smart girl, pretty tight,' Mihir smiles naughtily.

'No no. You can describe her at length. She is not your Bhabhi,' Uday says mischievously.

'He sounds like such a Casanova. He is like a typical Leo in this regard also,' Mihir says with a sense of fraternity. 'I am done. We should get going.'

'It is only 9.15. We can stay longer,' Uday says persuasively.

'And what about you? I know for sure you are having some serious affair. You are a keen birdwatcher but I have noticed the contentment in your eyes,' Uday says to Sandeep.

'Okay, I guess I should let both of you know. I am sort of guarded with my Ranchi friends since some of them know my family and they can be nasty enough to tell my already-scared father, who thinks Delhi will make an untamed bull out of his son. If he finds out about this, he will think I am not focusing on getting through the exams. He is crazy about his son being an IAS officer,' Sandeep explains.

'Okay Sandy, don't beat around the bush. Who is she, which college, how did it all start, how is it that if she is in the same college I have not met her?' Mihir floods him with questions.

'Don't you want to watch the movie? Okay then, let us drop the movie if you are keener on me than on your Bachchan,' Sandeep teases Mihir.

'The movie plan is on but you will not be spared so easily,' Uday says, intent on getting the story out of Sandeep.

'Yes, we can hear it on the way,' Mihir says.

'She is from Daulat Ram college. I met her for the first time during our college festival. She had come there with Shruti, a girl from Ranchi. I kept meeting her later also. We both began liking each other. It was pretty gradual actually. Her name is Aparna. She is certainly not the Delhi kind of girl and is more homely,' Sandeep says, feeling relieved at telling his friends and apprehensive about it going any further.

'Aha! Homely, you say! Looks like things have already advanced,' Uday says casually.

'Yes, of course we are serious. We want to get married but not now because my father would kill me. My Bade Bhaiya would just massacre me since he was already against my coming to Delhi. That is why I want to keep everything as secretive as possible.'

Mihir and Uday notice Sandeep's face turn sombre, though he forces himself to smile. By this time they have reached Batra and Uday goes to the counter. Mihir and Sandeep buy some chewing gum and cigarettes in the meanwhile. When Uday returns with the tickets he says solemnly, 'Sandeep, you have made this into a senti movie,' but his support is evident in his tone.

'Come on let's go and watch "Jumma Chumma". Bachchan is his usual magical self and has out-danced the new lot,' Sandeep says, trying to dispel the heaviness he feels he has cast upon them.

'This is why my funda is clear. I don't get into the adjective business—legend, great, phenomenal, par excellence, etc., I just make it plain and simple—Bachchan Boss,' Uday proclaims.

After the movie Uday guides the others through a shortcut that goes from behind the theatre.

'You are absolutely right; the man is matchless,' Mihir says, placing his hand on Sandeep's back. Mihir is reveling in the thought of his Kirori Mal connection with Amitabh Bachchan. Sandeep says to Uday, 'Hey this is truly a good shortcut. We have almost reached.'

'This is the popular Hanuman Temple that the inhabitants of this place throng on Tuesdays, especially the exam crowd,' Uday airs his knowledge of the place.

'You mean they trade on hope as well? The peda and boondi business must be thriving,' Sandeep says humorously as he yawns.

'What a keen sense of business it is. They know conquering a fucking demon like CS will require none less than the powerful Hanuman. Worshipping Him bestows the hope soma that keeps one high enough to face the demon with courage. Hanuman, high on real soma, gulped down the sun itself, leave alone fighting the demons. Hinduism takes care of all kinds and all occasions,' Mihir says philosophically.

Before Mihir could revel in his smartness, Uday roars, 'And what about the occasion of fucking? Don't we have a Kama Deva also?'

'You have taken care of your fucking Casanova self, but what about Mihir, who is the hide-and-seek kind? Let me tell you, even for that there is a God—Krishna, who stops at dalliances,' Sandeep joins in.

'Both of you are wrong. It's not Lord Krishna but Lord Shiva. Don't you think Jyoti is like Parvati chasing Shiva?' Mihir says with rare exuberance. Lord Shiva always stirs Mihir into a bizarre ecstasy that is beyond belief and doubt, bhakti and reason.

'And Sandy, what about you?' Mihir asks jovially.

'Lord Rama, loyal to one woman,' Uday says spontaneously.

'I just told you Hinduism takes care of every kind. At times I wonder whether our pantheon describes the unseen Gods or the seen humanity! It has characters of all sorts,' Mihir sounds philosophical.

'Man, it is simple. The Gods can't describe themselves, they have left it to man to describe them,' Uday says sarcastically.

'Uday never fails to settle his scores with God,' Sandeep says playfully.

The silence of the night is echoing with bonhomie as they enter their new flat and call it a day.

~

Settling into the Dream

As their home is settled, they get down to settling into their CS dreams.

'I don't think we can afford to regularly attend the PG classes. They take up too much time. We have to figure something out,' Mihir says. The three of them are sitting in the front room, having tea.

'Even I am a little worried. Settling into this house has taken time and now it's these PG classes,' Uday echoes.

'Yes, a balancing act is needed. Then again, we do need the minimum attendance.' Sandeep balances the concerns expressed by Mihir and Uday. Sandeep is more serious than the others about completing his MA.

'I know we need attendance. What I am more worried about is just getting through the PG course.' Mihir knows where Sandeep is going with his reference to attendance.

'Don't worry about that. I have already spoken to my Hansraj College friends. They are keen on MA. They have the latest tutes (the popular term for the notes of a senior),' Uday says.

'It is good that we opted for a specialization in Medieval instead of Modern. We would have gone crazy tracking the new research on the freedom struggle. Subaltern is the latest stir in the nationalist view of the freedom struggle. People are constantly digging out facts to prove how many local struggles were actually autonomous and not even known to Gandhi. They are the "people's struggles" that undermine Gandhi's absolute hegemony. Even the local tehsils and thanas are being excavated for this,' Sandeep says, pushing Mihir to debate with him.

'In Modern we are always judged by how many such research papers have been referred to,' Uday supports Sandeep.

'But the freedom struggle forms a major part of the portion for the CS exam also. Leaving our History optional aside, Medieval History is not needed in GS at all. Sometimes I think we should've picked Modern History instead because those finds would serve a dual purpose of helping for GS and the History optional as well,' Mihir says, the exams back at the front of his mind.

'No, in the CS exam you are not supposed to get too much into History. They say it should be plain, simple and straight, toeing the NCERT line, and you know that means the nationalist view. Any critique of Gandhi is nothing less than sacrilege when you are worshipping this Supreme God,' Sandeep argues.

'Yes. Who dares to write that more has been attributed to Gandhi than he actually deserved. "Pressure from below" is the latest fad. The fact remains that challenging any tradition has its own thrill because there are instant buyers for something sensational,' Uday says with authority. Both Mihir and Sandeep know that Uday has civil servants in his family which puts him on a pedestal for worshippers of civil services.

'But why be scared of new facts? They don't take anything away from Gandhi. That he was a great leader and his contribution to the freedom struggle is unmatched, doesn't change because of the "people's struggles". Why do we tend to attribute everything to the most powerful person, comfortably forgetting that even a little from others may have been critical in crossing the threshold?' Mihir says passionately.

'Even that point is hazardous,' Uday intervenes.

'But the exam for the civil services is the most prestigious in the country. Will it stand for the thwarting of reason and research that might be contrarian to tradition, especially when the subalterns are basing their contention on facts that can't be challenged? History cannot be the hegemony of a few and like any discipline or science it has to evolve with time. The discovery of new realities brings new truths. I admit that if one is focused on a particular truth and they dig out only those facts that prop up their truth, that is a different issue altogether.' Mihir sounds perplexed about how to approach the subject because he always wants to put forward new views in his answers.

Uday is worried that the debate between Mihir and Sandeep will go on for too long again, eating away their time. 'My dear friend! Don't go adrift. Cheers to Bipan Chandra. "Gandhi was a bourgeoisie leader", "Gandhi exercised undue control over the freedom struggle", "Subaltern struggles", let all these remain under the carpet of the theory that Gandhi wanted to protect the freedom struggle from class rifts and violence. Can you take the risk of putting down Gandhi and saying he called the movements off because he was scared of losing his control over the struggle? Just be safe and toe the nationalist line,' Sandeep says.

'I still will not take anything away from Gandhi. We must

concede that first he was a man. The feeling of power is inherent to man. So what if in a fit of power he went overboard and called the movements off? Why do we tend to seek perfection in a great man? In our desperate search for God, we tend to turn good into God, thrilled at bringing God amongst us,' Mihir again starts one of their constant discussions about Gods. 'Tired of our search for soma, we make Gods out of man. That man can unmake God we all know; the poor Moon God is lying trampled in the sky, not worshipped anymore.'

'So you are seriously focused now at establishing that Gandhi deliberately shackled the freedom movement under his hegemony?' Uday asks, unable to resist the temptation of the debate.

'You aren't understanding what I am saying. I don't know the truth, but what if Gandhi felt tempted to control the freedom struggle which he articulated and sculpted it to ultimate potency? Whether Subhas Chandra Bose was irrationally set aside or not will remain in history but the debate should continue. It is the root of growth. Let me put this simply, in spite of "Bose vs Gandhi", "calling off movements autocratically", etc., Gandhi remains the tallest leader of the country,' Mihir gives his opinion. In his mind he thinks, 'How come they sound so authoritative about the exams when I am so confused? There is probably something lacking in me.'

Uday is desperate to conclude the debate, 'Beware of turning intel (intellectual) and eating into precious time. Anyway Medieval is now frozen and I have also arranged tutes for that.'

Mihir is still thinking, 'Nothing succeeds like success. Those who have crossed this bloody sea of CS will have to be heard on the art and science of navigation. Uday is like the priest who too is deified for knowing God.'

Uday continues looking at Sandeep. 'About doing MA my funda is clear. Getting through is my ultimate goal. Getting attendance is crap and there is no point in wasting time on classes. They are meant for the intel kind.'

Sandeep's expression does not match his nod to Uday's proposal and he says, 'Yes we can go only for the critical classes, subjects that are absolutely new to us, like West Asian History.'

Uday sarcastically replies, 'He will just not get out of his MA. West Asia!'

'It's okay, attending a few classes is not a big deal. But even I have heard that tutes will be sufficient. One just has to devote half a day to most of the papers. The MA exams are held in the afternoon,' Mihir tries to mediate between Sandeep and Uday.

'What are your plans for the second optional subject for the exam?' Mihir asks Uday.

'I have decided on Pub. Ad. (public administration). I have some of my older cousin's study material,' Uday says confidently.

'As of now, I am torn between Anthropology and Geography,' Mihir says. 'At this point I feel completely lost. How can we be expected to cram a new subject of graduation level in a few months, especially something that is meant to be learnt over three years? Have you seen the syllabus? All the subjects demand graduate-level proficiency. Doesn't that seem absolutely weird?'

'That is exactly what it is, weird and wild. Weird, thy name is CS,' Uday says to lighten the atmosphere.

'I think we can settle on Geography. I know two of my friends who wrote their mains with Geography. I believe they can be of some help,' Sandeep says.

Mihir, slightly calmer after Uday's joke, says, 'That sounds good to me. Maps may fetch us full marks and Geography interested me in school as well.'

'Okay, that can wait. What about the prelims? That is the immediate poison. I know many people who braced for the mains and flunked in the prelims. We don't even need to go too far, Mihir. Rohit Singh of KMC? They vouched for his written skills and we vied for his grad tutes but he could not even get to writing the mains,' Sandeep says.

'I have made a strategy for this. My cousin vouches for group studies for prelims. We apportion the textbooks amongst a group for the notes and start solving as many test papers as possible. That way we can catch up on the difficult questions that the prelims often throws up. It sounds like a fantastic strategy to me. What do you think?' Uday says sanctimoniously.

'I also think the idea is practical. More than anything else it will make the difficult look a bit easier. Sort of lubricate the screw. A sense of compulsion because of the involvement of many will also help,' Mihir agrees.

'Yes. In fact it is perfect,' Sandeep says happily, sensing an opportunity to attend more MA classes in the distributed efforts.

'So we must get started right away with the book distribution and preparation of notes. There is an ARSD (college) guy living in 860 (House No.), just behind us, part of the Patna fraternity, with another CS guy who wrote his mains this year. They are keen on joining in.' Uday brings order to the chaos.

'So why not apportion the share this evening itself?' Mihir proposes.

'Yes. We can get started with making the prelims type objective notes which we can share amongst ourselves when the group studies begin. First we will cram and then we can do the practice lessons,' Uday says.

'What about GS? Do you remember Rajiv Verma at Sudhir's party? He said we need to study "everything under the sun"!' Mihir reminds them. 'The study of Science and Maths up to our intermediate will help, I believe. We will cram the History and Geography NCERTs anyway. For Indian Constitution we have D.D. Basu anyway. We can cut out relevant articles from newspapers and pool them. The NBT handbooks will help for Art and Culture and the guides are there for everything else.'

'*The Hindu* is a must. I have heard its supplement on science, technology and the economy is fabulous,' Sandeep contributes.

'We can do group studies again. It will work even better for GS,' Uday says.

'Shit! It's dinner time. Even a bit of Gandhi Baba invariably makes us tipsy. The fellow never fails to brew soma. Where is Bahadur?' Uday asks.

'No, no. He will come for sure but he is late because he has to finish his work in 960 first. They have some guests today and wanted their dinner early,' Sandeep explains.

'Even if he doesn't come we shouldn't worry. Cheers to Maggi and eggs,' Mihir says. 'I think we should be going to Batra to check for the Reddy's guides. It's the time for our customary evening excursion anyway. Bahadur knows where we keep the keys.'

'Yes, enough of this. Let's bird-watch at Batra for new arrivals,' Uday gets up excitedly.

'Let us go. Bahadur will clear the mess,' Sandeep points at the cups and plates by the bed.

'Hi Mr Tidy! You are out to catch all the birds with your neat looks,' Sandeep calls to Sudhir at the paan shop behind the magazine stall at Batra.

'Hello guys! How are you liking this place? All settled?' Sudhir asks Mihir and Sandeep.

'Yes, almost! What about your preparations?' Sandeep asks.

'I will just be back.' Uday spots some boys across the lane. 'Ajit is there. I will meet him and get back in a while. He is the ARSD chap I mentioned sometime back. I will talk to them about the group study plan'.

'Okay,' Sudhir says. 'Leave preparation aside for now. Enjoy some real glitter.' Sudhir points to a group of luscious lasses, local residents of MN. One of the girls, the tallest of the lot, is wearing a patiala salwar suit and is really pretty. She has big eyes highlighted by kajal, her eyes looking for the attention she knows is there. She blushes when she notices them. The neon light over her head lends her a celestial hue. Even Mihir glances at her from time to time.

'Really out of the world!' Sandeep says to Mihir. 'What about her, Mihir? Feeling a bit stirred up now?' Sandeep asks, brightened up with mischief.

'He is too much. He couldn't encash Jyoti's bold advances. The poor girl could not have been bolder. I hope everything is okay with him,' Sudhir says sarcastically.

'Not again! We're back to Jyoti? You people are so fixated on her, you embarrass me,' Mihir says, getting conscious.

Mihir's handling of his desire is complex. He is used to getting attention and advances from girls but he never responds. He can't decide whether he is incapable of responding or if his ego is satiated just by the attention and the pleasure of spurning the advances. Whatever the complex that is depriving him of indulging in his desire, at times he thinks it is pathological.

'This is Ajit, my friend from Patna who used to live in my locality. This is Alok who wrote his civil services mains. They now intend to be our screw mates,' Uday introduces the friends he went to talk to, enacting the 'screw' with booming laughter.

'We were just bathing in the dazzle of a blushing beauty,' Sudhir explains.

'Without me?' Uday turns to look at the girl.

'Just look there. That guy with the girl behind him on the bike is an IIT chap. Last year he had a different one, a localite. He got into the IAS this year in his first attempt. He doesn't talk much, keeps to himself and lives alone in a barsati on top of a flat near the MN bus stop. I am really impressed with the élan with which he carries on both the flings together. He doesn't believe in getting into the hanky-panky of a senti affair,' Ajit says with an "I-wish-I-was-him" expression on his face.

'The guy has the best of both the worlds,' Sandeep says, conscious of his own affair, serious and sentimental.

As Sandeep, Ajit and Alok start talking to Uday, Sudhir draws Mihir away from the group and asks, 'What do you think of that chap?' while pointing to an unassuming-looking guy, with a rustic demeanour and lost eyes, probably dazzled by the openness and freedom. 'What do you think this fresh arrival must be thinking? "I have not lost sight of my goal, I'm not cheating my parents and squandering their money. I am capable of self-restraint, etc.?' No way! He is probably wishing he had access to the girl so he could instantly climb to climax. Can't you tell from his starved looks? In just a few days this Panditji will first get his tikki chopped off, then buy a pair of boot-cut denims and tight-fit T-shirts with high-ankle boots and a new look. I can already see the aspiration on his face. Look at how he is smiling in complete bewilderment, caught up in the fantasy of something exciting happening to him. Do you think that this eternally squinting Panditji can ever train his eyes in meditation on attaining the CS God?

'And you, God knows what stuff you are made of, not eating out of the palate of desire laid out before you,' Sudhir finally finishes talking.

Mihir tries to figure out the resemblance between him and the Pandit. 'Don't I also want something exciting to happen to me as well? In my case it is my confusion that gets in the way.'

'This hapless species writhing in envy at the biker lot is mostly imported from Bihar, propping up this flourishing economy.' Sudhir points his hand at the different shops. 'I know of many who are neither here nor there, who lose both worlds and go home empty-handed. You know we are masters at making traditions out of our needs and so even this exile has become a fad. "His son at Delhi has got through civil services" is like Ganesha drinking milk everywhere. Since his Ganesha has drunk milk mine will too.'

Mihir listens to Sudhir and thinks, 'Will this Panditji ever get through the civil services exams?' Mihir tries to mould him into Sudhir's sketch but stops before a big 'no' could spring up, hitting him hard.

'You sound too smug about your achievements, don't you think? I am yet to see any lass by your side or is that a secret?' Mihir turns his attention to Sudhir.

'So far no one. Falling head over heels for a girl is beyond me. But of course, even if an ambiguous advance lurks, I will go fishing.'

'Sudhir is overestimating his appearance,' Mihir can't help thinking unkindly.

Sudhir, Mihir and the other boys move towards their respective haunts without breaking their conversations.

'You carry on. I will just follow you in a bit. I have to buy a few things from the store,' Mihir says.

As Mihir is rejoining the group he is thinking, 'It is a world of fiery ambition, furious attitude and frenzied endeavour juxtaposed against a lethal coupling of freedom and flaming desire. But I have to strike a balance. Nothing can sway me from my path to achieve my ambition.'

A few thoughts are emerging in his mind.

Thought 1

My father is sitting in the verandah conducting tuitions for added resources. He has to send a sizeable amount for these Delhi classes. He didn't save too much because he was providing for his parents and brothers.

Thought 2

Both my sisters are of marriageable age; the elder one on the wrong side of it. My father doesn't have the resources to get them married. My mother is eternally worried about her failure to earn the satisfaction of managing her daughters' marriages and the uncertainties involved in her son's settlement. I have already forsaken my admission in an engineering college and everyone in Sitagarh has huge expectations. Hers is a small world and people know her family well. She aspires to get her daughters married and her son settled.

Thought 3

My father's reputation has to match his social achievements. So I have to leave no stone unturned on my path to CS to increase the prestige of the family. I have to justify his eternal support for my ambitions. The services are the ultimate consummation of academic excellence in our world at Sitagarh and this way I can repay the sacrifices my father has made.

Thought 4

I am a role model for my peers who emulate me and have flocked to Delhi. They think my company itself may be rewarding. Thus I need to get into the civil services.

Gradually the trio settles into business, following the strategy they have devised. Evening tea sessions are customary for them. That is when they review what they have done and how they are progressing. It has been a month since they have gotten into the groove.

'How far are you done with your Bipan Chandra?' Uday asks Mihir.

'I am almost halfway through. I would've gotten through more but I got curious about the subaltern view of Gandhi and started Sumit Sarkar. The freedom struggle never fails to fascinate me.'

'What about you, Sandy?' Uday asks.

'Frankly speaking, I haven't finished much. Two chapters

of Medieval in *Three Authors*,' Sandeep's reply does not surprise Uday or Mihir.

Mihir smiles, 'Sandy is feasting on his MA.'

'Sandy! That is just not allowed,' Uday says.

'Listen to me you two. For our MA we have to watch out not only for West Asia but for Ancient Civilizations as well. We have not studied this earlier,' Sandeep says, unable to hide the guilt in his voice.

'No matter what, he manages to come up with a guise for his MA,' Uday says.

Mihir's gaze switches between Sandeep and Uday. 'I often see him walking out of the campus through the Daulat Ram gate, notebook under his arm. At the exit he lights up his cigarette, *Deewar's* Bachchan style, to smoke in contentment after an absorbing session,' Mihir says. Uday and Mihir are both a bit worried about the schedule they have chalked out.

'The more we lag behind in finishing our notes, the more we drift apart in our group studies,' Uday says sombrely. 'Okay, 15 September is our deadline. No matter what we have to finish our notes by then.'

'Sure,' Sandeep yields instantly, knowing that it is the preparation for the exams that has brought them together and a deflection from the rituals would be nothing less than sacrilege. 'I have a major announcement to make. Mihir is already in the group studies. That way, he will be doubling it up,' Sandeep says, with a mysterious smile.

'What do you mean by that?' Mihir asks, confused.

'The market is already abuzz with the news. I am only the messenger. They say Mihir and Jyoti are finally together now. They have been studying together in the central reference library,' Sandeep says, looking playfully at Uday.

'Mihir! What is this secrecy? Even Sherlock Holmes would not be able to tell. This prep is getting the better of me but I am happy that I am finally rubbing off on you. Okay now prepare yourself because you are under the eternal watch of this Sherlock Holmes,' Uday says excitedly.

'No way! Don't pull things out of nowhere. It is just that she also comes there to study. I have not even spoken to her, leave alone being together with her. If you want to indulge in gossip, I don't mind though because it does provide respite from the prep boredom,' Mihir says, unable to hide the blush on his cheeks.

He thinks, 'Am I telling the truth or am I lying? I feel a sense of togetherness without us being together. I want to speak to her but I also don't want to. I want to know her but I also don't want to.' Mihir ejects himself from the Mona Lisa hue.

'Looks like Mihir is rebelling against himself. The scene begins!' Sandeep is at his mischievous best, looking for a way to display his theatrics. Even Mihir is wondering what will eventually unfold. Sandeep begins, 'Our brother walks out dressed to kill; boot-cut jeans flaring over his shiny shoes, unbuttoned shirt hugging his body, his bag packed with his prep material. He reaches the library and gets a chair which is pretty much earmarked for him and starts scanning his books. In half an hour he packs up and walks out in a huff, screaming, "No! No! No! What is happening to me? I am succumbing to her attraction and she is tearing my concentration to shreds. I cannot take it anymore. I am not coming back tomorrow onwards." He throws his bag down with an angry thud. This happened last Thursday. But the library mission is still on.'

Mihir is left embarrassed and shy and Sandeep revels in his embarrassment, looking vengefully smug at punishing him for being the witness to his MA crime. The ambience is reverberating with a boisterous camaraderie.

'Oh no! How do you know all this? Were you there?' Mihir is confused. Uday, till now a mute spectator, finally says, 'Mihir, it is now or never. Just take a short dip and leave before any sentimental thing gets in the way. Take the word of an experienced guy who is a pro at dabbling in desire without any side-effects—managing girls is a craft. It is medicinal. Sandy is a class apart, getting his motivation from being sentimental.'

Sandeep says, 'Let us accompany him on his mission.'

'Before that you have to tell us how you found all this out. If you were not around who told you? Was it Sanjit?'

'Yes, it was him, your Hansraj friend,' Sandeep reveals. 'But no harm can come to my informer. It is the rule of the game.'

Uday excitedly jumps up and grips Mihir, embracing him and asking for more details, 'There is no escape now. You have to tell us everything.'

Mihir says, 'But I need to breathe to talk!'

'Fine fine,' Uday says, releasing him.

'You already know the KMC thing pretty well. Sandeep was the one who rescued me on that fateful day I was ragged and that is when I met Jyoti. I never knew she would take that odd meeting so seriously with the constant exchange of gazes. She started coming to the library almost a week after me. Naturally we both fell into the routine of silent attraction. In the library she sits in the inner section across the glass and my eyes, though buried in my books, can sense her stares. She compels me into watching her, as if scolding me for not returning her gaze. She then suddenly looks at her books when she sees me looking back at her. When I don't budge, she stands up and moves from one shelf to another, feigning a frantic search for some book, brushing my desk with her long skirt as she passes by, as if to assault my concentration. Even a whiff of her perfume leaves me completely distracted and she sets my heart aflutter with a strange excitement. She even matches her coffee timings with mine. She walks with a springy gait that turns springier when I am around. In short, she has cast her spell on all my library outings, and that day when I realized it, I left in a huff.' Mihir blushes furiously.

'Damn! If something like that ever happened to me I would immediately chase her. You are a lucky man,' Uday says passionately.

Mihir suddenly finds Uday's words and expressions not sitting well; a sense of possessiveness rising against his words.

'Let him be. He will never mend his ways, incorrigible narcissist that he is,' Sandeep says with resignation, looking at Uday.

Mihir thinks, 'Alas! If I could just lose myself to desire! But what if unlike Sandy and Uday I can't strike a balance. Sandy has managed his emotions and Uday is gifted with the talent of dabbling in desire without any side-effects.'

~

Harries in Exile

Making a strategy is exciting but following it through is a pain. The strict regimen that the preparation strategy demanded gradually saps the trio's bonhomie; the ensuing prelims is casting a shadow of sombreness over their lives. It is the end of September. Group studies have begun in Ajit's roommate Alok's flat. This choice was made with no planning.

In the world of MN, identities are defined by how far through the civil services process the people are. For example, prelims-through, mains-through, CS cracker etc. The prestige is added to the identity with a number. For example, thrice prelims-through, twice mains-through, etc. Every step affords attention, respect and awe. The biker chap from IIT cracking his exam in the first go is a flash of magic.

Mihir, Uday and Sandeep reach Ajit's place in the afternoon after their siesta and tea. On the first day, things are more focused around planning the modalities and the scheduling of the subjects. The first few weeks involve cramming and then each day of the six-day week has been allotted one topic followed by practice tests. Alok, who has cleared prelims, says a few words, accorded the privilege his identity demands. Uday is smug in the fact that he facilitated the group studies and the air is filled with an exciting sense of contentment but not without a throbbing sense of apprehension. The sense of working towards a common goal brings them together.

'I think this is enough for today. Tomorrow we can get started with Ancient History. First we learn everything that we have studied and then the supplementary,' Alok says.

'Now let's enjoy some tea and I have some homemade mixture of flattened rice and chana dal,' Ajit says, taking on the role of a good host.

The next day they all assemble on time. The cramming affair proceeds with passion.

Twenty days later, the practice test session begins.

'Which is the most recent site of the Indus Valley civilization?' Alok asks the group. The dice is handed first to Ajit, sitting immediately next to Alok, Uday being on the other side. Ajit reclines on his side, his legs folded, his ear balanced on his palm, his brows furrowed with effort. Overall the picture that emerges is that of a person looking into infinity, contemplating the answers to the mysteries of the universe.

Ajit is of medium height with a dusky complexion. His bulging hips and belly give him a rotund appearance. He talks with an extra thrust of the tongue behind certain syllables, a camouflage for his slight stammer.

'Lothal?' Ajit asks, with his trademark emphasis on 'L' in Lothal.

'Rakhigarhi,' everyone says in a chorus.

Gradually the boys realize Ajit's penchant for forgetting

what has been crammed just a while back. Ajit's appearance of being in a trance, his wrong answers, and his self-deprecating regret all make him a person who generates instant humour and invites ridicule, though all in bonhomie and good fun.

'Can't recall, Ajit may answer,' is a running joke in the group whenever a break is needed. Uday is pretty adept at mimicking Ajit in a trance and tends to imitate him even in the thick of a session, mostly in front of Sandeep, sparking generous laughter.

'What happened? I want to know,' Ajit asks despite knowing what they are making fun of. When ridiculed, feigning ignorance is a natural reflex.

However, Mihir, who is more sensitive than the others, feels a prick in his heart every time he sees an embarrassed Ajit.

'Enough! Let us get back. Alok, are we on the right track?' Mihir finds ways to divert attention from Ajit, who can sense empathy. Gradually Mihir realizes that Ajit is looking for an opportunity to catch him alone. Empathy naturally attracts him towards Mihir.

'I don't know what to do. Whatever I study either doesn't enter my brain at all or escapes as soon as it enters,' Ajit explains to Mihir on the one afternoon he finally succeeds in catching Mihir alone in his flat. Mihir doesn't enquire nor does Ajit have to explain the context.

'It happens to many. Maybe you just need to study more to be able to remember,' Mihir tries pacifying Ajit.

'But then it has always been like this. It is why I could never score well in any of my exams so far. I sometimes feel like banging my head against a wall and cursing God,' Ajit says emotionally.

'Who says high scores in your previous exams are mandatory

for CS? I have definitely come across many like you who have cracked CS. Passion has the power to tide over man's frailties no matter how deep-rooted they are,' Mihir says.

'At least those people manage to retain something when they concentrate hard. Not like me who still can't get a hold on myself. I believe I should have stuck to my Company Secretaryship,' Ajit says reflectively.

'Company Secretaryship? You were enrolled for that?' Mihir is surprised.

'Yes. I have done my B.Com from ARSD college. After Class 12, my father virtually coaxed me to shift to Delhi. If it isn't a distraction for you, let me tell you the whole story.'

'Sure, I'm all ears,' Mihir says. A creature of the mind himself, Mihir is excited to enter the realm of Ajit's psyche.

'We are five brothers and two sisters and I'm the youngest of all. My eldest brother, who is about twelve years older, jumped into the JP movement started by Jayaprakash Narayan. You're from Bihar so you must be aware of the sweep of the JP movement. It took Bihar by storm and later moved even to Delhi. It was a student movement because of the sheer number of students who participated in it. You remember the slogan, "*Poora anaaj, poora kaam, nahin to hoga chakka jam*"? It whipped the students into a frenzy against unemployment and corruption. Caught in that trap, he ruined his career and couldn't even complete his graduation. The students had boycotted classes and colleges had come to a standstill; no exams could be held and academic sessions had no meaning. My brother, like many others, was infected by netagiri. So my father asked me to come here to Delhi and finish my graduation. He told me to pursue whatever I wanted. I was an average student but keen to do better than my brothers and my father felt very sad that none of his sons could do anything worthwhile, so he wanted me to do something. That is why I am here. Knowing my limitations, I enrolled myself into the Company Secretaryship course. But once here I found everyone worshipping the other CS, the civil services. I felt left out and living with Alok, who had already cleared his prelims, made me change my mind. I am still enrolled in my diploma course though. They are very flexible and give ample time to complete the course. So here I am with you, struggling with myself as always.'

'It is absolutely fine that you are making an attempt at the better CS. You have nothing to lose. Your diploma can wait. But once you are cast in this ocean, stay afloat for some time before taking a final call,' Mihir counsels Ajit, taken up by a rush of empathy.

Mihir wonders whether his advice is sane or just a compassionate gesture to calm Ajit since the guy seems to have bitten off more than he can chew. Mihir again ejects himself out of his thoughts to escape from the discomfiture.

'Okay, I should go now. I have taken up too much of your time. Thank you for letting me share my feelings with you. I feel much better, even though things haven't changed. See you in the afternoon,' Ajit says on his way out.

Mihir mulls over how Ajit has just explained the main reasons for the migration of students from Bihar to Delhi. Some snapshots are flashing in Mihir's mind. He remembers himself as a small boy on the streets of Sitagarh watching a crowd of students frenziedly shouting, *'Poora anaaj, poora kaam, nahin to hoga chakka jam'*. The sight of the students swarming the streets was growing frequent. To Mihir they appeared to be gripped more by revelry and mass hysteria than disgruntlement. This was just one of the many such scenes occasioned by the visit of Jayaprakash Narayan, who had risen in revolt against the regime of Indira Gandhi on the issues of corruption and the deteriorating health of democracy. This is what Mihir remembers learning from his father. Mihir vividly remembers to have witnessed the two mammoth public meetings JP held. Mihir's memories that were stirred up by the conversation with Ajit are now being connected to the world Mihir has landed in. He realizes that most of them are in Delhi probably because of the problems in Bihar. That state, despite the JP movement, is still a symbol of everything wrong with the country—poverty, backwardness, illiteracy, poor infrastructure and education. Students from Bihar hide their identity for no fault of theirs, backward migrants in their own country. Mihir is suddenly reminded of Santosh from Betia, his classmate from KMC, who claimed to be from Punjab; he gave his maternal uncle's Ambala address as his in the admission form. Mihir is now growing conscious of the times he aggressively exhibited his sophistication when he was around non-Biharis just to prove that Harries, a derogatory term for people from Bihar, cannot all be judged derogatively. A mundane incident with darker undertones from a few days back comes to the fore of his mind.

Mihir, Uday and Sandeep were awakened early in the morning after a long night by some loud shouts from outside, 'You bloody Biharis are all so ill-mannered and uncivilized!' Sandeep ready to fight, shouted, 'Who is this abusing us Harries so boldly? Let me go out and find out.'

'Wait, let me come with you. Let me also see who is making so much noise,' Uday chipped in, the sleeves of his T-shirt rolled up to show off his biceps. 'Mihir! Come, Bihar's prestige is at stake.'

'Sure, I'm coming,' Mihir said with his characteristic soft aggression.

They went out to see a middle-aged hefty man standing in the front balcony of the flat just adjacent to theirs, banging on the door of the first-floor flat.

The three stood outside in the verandah and noticed that their landlord's son, Sonu, had also come down.

'That is Gulati Uncle. He lives in the house next to the flat he is in. He is a pakka khadoos and is always scowling,' Sonu told them.

'Yes, even I see him standing in front of his house in the evening,' Sandeep replied angrily.

Then a boy opened the door of the flat and came out.

'Yes Uncle? What is the issue, why are you shouting?' Two more boys came out of the house.

'Shouting! Me? Just look at you rascal Biharis. What were you all doing last night playing the music so loudly as if the world didn't exist?' the man screamed with contempt in his eyes.

'Mind your tongue, Uncle. Don't bring Bihar into the issue and don't talk this way. Last night we had a party. It doesn't happen all the time.' The boy tried to control his anger.

'Have your parents sent you all this way to party or study? You Bihar children are all wasting your parents' money. In Bihar parents don't teach their children manners. What were you saying? Me, minding my tongue? A rascal will be called a rascal,' the man continued to scream.

Sandeep was ready to join the argument but Uday and Mihir held him back.

'Uncle, enough is enough. We will not keep listening to your trash,' the boy charged forward but his flatmates stopped him. 'We know what we are doing. You don't need to sermonize about our studies. I have already been selected into the Delhi Police force as an ACP. If the music disturbed you, we're sorry; but then we have to bear a lot of things too. Your children play cricket right in the middle of the road every day. You organize your weddings and birthday parties on the road, blocking it for hours together, but do we object? I understand that it is common human tendency to not bother when we cause inconvenience but to get angry when we are inconvenienced.'

'You Biharis never listen. If we get together against you...' the man threatened and charged forward in a huff.

'Enough with the name-calling, Uncle,' Sandeep screamed from the balcony. 'Don't be under the illusion that we are in your den. As for how we Biharis are studying, most of the ACPs and DCPs who scare you are Biharis. Didn't you hear? Even this boy is now a part of the Delhi Police. He is writing his UPSC again and may even get into the IPS to drive a fatter bamboo into...' he enacted the rest of his words to convey his intended meaning.

By then many people had gathered around.

'Let me tell you, the Delhi kudis are attracted to Biharis like iron filings to magnets, not to your mundays,' Uday said while making deliberately rude gestures, inviting the man to engage.

'Uncle, we are not here for a Bihar vs Delhi battle but you are rubbing us the wrong way by calling us rascals,' Mihir said. He tends to sound rational and philosophical even on such occasions.

The man was now overwhelmed by the aggression of the

boys. But overcoming his intimidation he countered, 'Then why do you all migrate to Delhi if you are so intelligent and studious?'

The boys visibly blanched on hearing his comment.

Mihir immediately replied, 'Uncle, do you know this entire colony of yours is called a refugee colony? The government gave you this land free to settle here. Why did you all migrate from erstwhile Punjab, now in Pakistan? You fled from post-Partition violence to save your life and in the same way we have fled from the poor state of education in Bihar to save our career. Delhi is as much ours as yours. Understood?'

Mihir's argument left Uday and Sandeep flushed with the radiance of victory. By now the others could sense the affair taking an ugly turn and murmurings to quieten things down erupted. 'Leave them alone. They have come to study. There is no point ruing the occasional fun they have. They are also our children,' an old sensible man said, taking the other man with him.

The boys, a little guilty about what happened, waved the crowd away saying, 'Sorry. We didn't intend to hurt anyone, but we were provoked.'

The trio went back to their flat and Sandeep said with some pain in his voice, 'Why is our Bihar left lying in shambles? We were born and brought up there. When anyone slights Bihar I feel my dear house and my lovely school all abused.'

'Even I get sad when many of us tend to hide our identities, I can also understand the latent pain in Biharis humorously calling themselves Harries,' Uday seconded.

Mihir now thinks of Santosh from 'Ambala', who is actually from Patna. 'Today one has to hide one's identity in one's own country.' Mihir goes back to bed, but suddenly begins thinking of the Mandal Commission instead of falling asleep. Tonight his mind is blazing again.

~

Flaming Desire

Mihir wakes up with a weak body and a fatigued mind. He usually feels like this when winter changes to spring. The sense of a strange stillness of the approaching summer and the rustling breeze make him gloomy. To Mihir the rhyme of spring is a dirge to the death of winter.

This morning is gloomier than the others, though. Mihir thinks, 'The MA exams are close and CS prelims are just after that. This is the only attempt I have that is free from the OBC reservation. Next year onwards the services will drift farther from me as they will probably reduce their intake too, further diminishing the probability of my getting in. Then again I am not equipped to crack CS in my first attempt. To me it is a way to get experience. Heck, I haven't even decided my second optional for mains.'

The enormity of the MA exams and prelims under the shadow of the implementation of the Mandal Commission looms on Mihir. Feeling comatose, he goes deeper into his mind. He decided not to go to the library and stays in bed.

His mind is still following the same train of thoughts. More snapshots from his past come to him—his walking into the Arts Faculty complex, slogans flooding the campus air, 'No reservations please', 'Please don't divide us', 'No caste politics please'. Suddenly, at a distance, a frenzied commotion erupts. The students, including Mihir, head to see what is happening. To his horror he sees a boy in flames. 'Hey! It is Rajiv from Deshbandhu College,' scream a few, even as others run for water and blankets. In a fit of horror Mihir leaves the crowd, feeling sick. As he is walking away he hears, 'These are the funeral pyres of meritocracy and an immolation of our ambitions.' At the exit, a boy stops Mihir and in a fit of frenzy says, 'You know, my roommate takes a flight to go home while I struggle for a berth in second class, and he is a beneficiary of reservations. Are they blind?' That night Mihir couldn't sleep; the night remained ablaze with heart-wrenching melancholia.

This morning, as the frightening implications of reservations loom large, Mihir feels guilty about being distant from the anti-reservations stir. He thinks, 'We tend to avoid the screw unless it stares right into our faces. Mihir remains lost in his thoughts, thinking , 'What if this MA–prelims combination could fly by, or if this doesn't arrive at all!' He shuts out the world and lets his thoughts play out, asleep and awake at the same time.

'Hey, aren't you going to the library?' Mihir feels his blanket being flung off his body. Uday is trying to wake him up.

'Nope, I'm not going today,' Mihir says.

'Are you not feeling well?' Uday asks, holding his breakfast plate in his hands.

'Yeah, I am feeling a little sick. March is normally harsh on me. My feet and palms start sweating, causing an imbalance of salt in my body and leaving me weak. It happens every year and it's nothing to worry about. The sweet-salty lemonade helps instantly. It will go away on its own,' Mihir says, reclined against the pillows. 'What are you up to?'

'I am going to Hansraj College today for the MA tutes.' Uday sits on the chair beside Mihir's bed. 'Sandy is already out. Probably for class.'

'Sandy's class notes will be a big help,' Mihir says sarcastically.

'He just refuses to budge from his MA, but thank God. At least he still completed the prelims work assigned to him,' Uday says.

'I think we now have to prepare for the whole hog,' Mihir says.

'We have finished History. We can manage Stats with our Plus Two Maths skills. We are already taking newspaper notes and my older cousin has given me some objective-type notes on NCERT Geography and the Indian Constitution. After Holi we can club GS with our History group study. Reddy's will be very important for GS since the practice tests will ease our cramming. Studying Science in Class 12 will be a vantage point for us to manage the General Science part of GS. Don't worry too much. We will get started in full swing after Holi,' Uday explains.

Uday's mention of Holi sparks instant excitement and dispels some of Mihir's gloom.

'God knows how Holi will unfold in this new place,' Mihir says sombrely, nostalgic about the last Holi, which he had spent with his parents.

'Man! The localites and the migrants together paint a riotous Holi! Don't worry too much. The Harries make it an exciting event. Several groups start simultaneously and finally converge at Batra to paint it in boisterous colours. There is a high from singing and dancing, over and above the free-flowing booze, and all the girls also join in. We can do some real feasting on those luscious dishes under the guise of Holi celebrations,' Uday shares his experiences.

'Then boys already in affairs with the local kudis must be having a fun time,' Mihir says with a tinge of envy.

'Man! You can also have fun! We should invite Jyoti to make it a complete affair for you,' Uday says mischievously.

'Not again! Does no other world exist beyond Jyoti?' Mihir says, visibly blushing.

'Okay, in that case, if you have someone other than Jyoti in mind for Holi flirtations, may I know who she is?' Uday tries to cheer Mihir up.

Mihir just smiles.

'Okay listen, I have something interesting to share with you,' Uday says, firing Mihir's curiosity. 'There is a boy from Patna, Mukesh, living nearby in a single room on the top floor. He's pretty rich and is quite the stud. He isn't very tall and he is here not because of his ambition but his money. He has been screwing his landlady at will. She is pretty tight and voluptuous and lives with her baby son. Her husband is in Dubai and it is rumoured he is having an affair with a Muslim woman. They are filthy rich and the lady is constantly lavishing Mukesh with gifts. What luck he has, he's being paid to screw!' Uday's jealousy is evident.

'The lady is no less lucky. She has everything—the financial security of a marriage without the sacrifice of the freedom which marriage normally demands, a satiation of her maternal instincts and, to top it all, the fulfilment of her urges without any moral compunctions,' Mihir says.

'Shit! I am late. I'll just make you some lemonade and then head out. I'm sure the story also must have done some good to you.'

'No, no. Don't worry about it. I will manage.'

'No way. Just wait. I'll be back in a few minutes.'

Mihir hears Uday bustling around, making a glass of lemonade for him. He is touched by how he remembered his need for lemonade through their conversations. Uday's revelations leaves Mihir writhing in lust, his mind eclipsed in the thoughts of the landlady. Alone in the house, Mihir tosses with desire, his solitude sending his mind into sinful imaginings. He starts thinking of Mukesh screwing his landlady, the raw oomph of a ripening woman and the untamed virility of raging youth crazily craving for each other in a lonely house... He instantly surrenders to a frenzied fantasy. Hiding under the blanket for privacy he lets his desires flow furiously.

Once relieved, a placid Mihir slides back into his melancholia. He writes in his diary with a sense of urgency, 'I am suspended, yet fixed, stilled in the turbulence of my mind. My thoughts emerge in a luscious stream, settling down into a sonorous rhyme. This moment, lying lifeless, I am pulsating with life. This is an uncategorized moment between two lives.' After he finishes, he turns the pages to go over his old entries. He hopes someday they will see the light of other minds and his dream to be a writer begins.

Released and relieved after a lazy morning, Mihir feels like jumping back into the CS world. Through with his morning chores, he makes himself some tea and eggs for breakfast. He finds the newspaper, which is holy for them now. The creases and smell of smoke tell him that Sandeep has already read them. 'SLR and CRR slashed to facilitate credit to the manufacturing sector', 'Tax holidays to promote exports', 'Excise slashed further to boost manufacturing'—the headlines greet Mihir's CS-accustomed eyes. The headlines bring Gandhi to his mind, in particular Hind Swaraj and Antodaya for the production for masses vs mass production. Realizing he has drifted off again, Mihir halts his train of thought. He looks out at the bustling street—a few people are going their way on bikes, bicycles, rickshaws etc. He can see inside a nearby school with a few children looking at the blackboard. Then he feels a prick of guilt at breaking his routine. It stirs his placidity. But then he thinks, 'Today there is no point in challenging what my heart feels. It is enjoying the break from routine. I will reignite the CS fire in me after Holi and it is only a matter of three more days.'

Suddenly the door opens with a bang, breaking Mihir out of his meditative slumber.

'I was just telling you this morning that Holi is going to be even more boisterous this time. On the way back I met a few Holi enthusiasts. They are planning to import Bihar's Holi with all its fun, and this time we have Jumma Chumma as well to drive everyone crazy.' Uday enters, his booming voice preceding him.

~

Jumma Chumma Holi

'Hey, have they arrived?' Mihir heads to the back of the house.

'Scared of getting coloured? That is what Holi is for. Come on!' Uday charges out, puffing himself while rolling up the sleeves of the kurta he is wearing specially for the day.

'Sandy! Come out of the bathroom, they are waiting outside,' Mihir prompts Sandeep. He then sees Sudhir who has been coloured so vehemently that even his eyes aren't visible through the colours on his face.

'Come out fast you two. Mihir lift the carton of beer onto the kitchen slab,' Uday says, simultaneously wishing Sudhir.

'Hurry up! We have to cover the whole of Mukherjee Nagar this time. No one can be spared,' Sudhir is already in a frenzy.

The trio, led by Sudhir, go out with Mihir and Sandeep, placing the carton of beer on a trailer rickshaw heaped with snacks and booze that has been specially hired for Holi. The cart is to be driven on a turn-by-turn basis and the first one to drive is Brijesh, Uday's erstwhile roommate, and an acclaimed leader of the booze bonhomie. Uday holds the packet of colours and designer Holi caps for the three of them. Sandeep instantly starts cheering, '*Holi hai bhai Holi hai. Bura na mano Holi hai*!' while wildly spraying fistfuls of colour everywhere. The trio instantly get catapulted into the frenzy. They are high on unlimited booze and unregulated bonhomie. The crowd marches on and no one knows who is colouring whom. Mihir, Sandeep and Uday are guzzling the beer to get more drunk. Sandeep rushes back and gets Brijesh to hand the rickshaw over to him. The crowd keeps swelling with new entrants.

At one of the squares, their group meets a group of girls, soberly boisterous and high on the attention raining upon them rather than because of Holi. A few exchange glances with the boys they know; with some it's flirtation and infatuation, in other cases attraction and relation. The group of girls consists of students and the local kudis who have made friends with their fellow tenants. They are moving in parallel or in tandem with the boys for whom it is a sheer bonanza. The girls are drenched in colours, their clothes almost one with their skin, accentuating their femininity to the fullest and affording the boys copious draughts of desire. In a short while, Sandeep and Uday huddle together and Sandeep who is very high says, 'Uday is missing his Sanjana. He has finally turned emotional.' He then shouts, 'What happened to your being master of your sentiments, dictating desire?' Then he turns to Mihir and says, 'This is your fate too. To let the head rule the heart is to spurn soma.'

The groups reach their final destination—Batra, their eternal haunt. The restaurants have already set up a supply of chicken and mutton biryani and paneer. The leaders of the groups have reached the centre of the crowd and it is understood that they will perform for the rest. Uday and Sandeep are in the centre, wildly swinging and swaying to the latest hit Bachchan song, jumma chumma de de, while fuelling themselves with the draughts of beer. Mihir, Ajit and Alok are standing in a line on the periphery, clapping and swaying.

Even in the crowd Mihir is lost in thought, 'This entire lot is captivated by soma. They are like Sufis in search of the same God, the civil services. The smugness from their knowledge that they are performing the dharma involving the most rigorous rites for attaining the Supreme God is driving them dizzy. They are high on the spirits of soma, kama, and dharma, and of course Bachchan.'

Suddenly Mihir feels a hand gripping his arm. It is Ajit taking him away from the horde. Mihir notices that Ajit is sombre and pensive. He says, 'Mihir! Come what may, once pushed into it, I will pull off the CS for sure.' Ajit has transformed from coward to conqueror. As he speaks Mihir thinks, 'Ajit is high on the mix of these spirits. This is revealing his innermost self which harbours the truth; the spirits douse the consciousness to illuminate the truth in man.'

Ajit suddenly bursts out singing, 'God CS de de, God CS de de, CS.'

~

Globetrotter Prof. Kapoor

After Holi, things settle down into a routine. The preparations for the services become more sober with each passing day as the prelims approach.

'How about attending some special classes for West Asia? Every year Prof. Kapoor takes special care of his students. He knows West Asia is tough and this way we can easily learn something which is a pain in the arse,' Sandeep proposes.

'In the thick of the prelims?' Uday asks, flustered. Mihir nods.

'But I am telling you, don't take a risk with West Asia. Even you both want to get through MA, don't you?' Sandeep asks, trying to scare them.

'Okay I saw last year's questions. The subject needs some hard work. Sandy makes sense. We should attend the socio-religious history part of it,' Mihir says.

'You mean like chewing gum? Gathering a little and elongating it as per the need?' Uday smiles, but the MA spilling over into the CS preparations is smothering his typical radiance. 'So finally we have to bear that hefty cowboy clad in his bermudas, tees and panama hat that he brought from California University. He consciously dons this look to attract girls, knowing that the West is still a USP in the East.'

'Yes, everybody knows that. Prof. Kapoor is constantly in search of his next prey,' Sandeep says. 'They say his special classes are an excuse to find some release for his urges.'

'How did you do find the class? Wasn't I correct—the multiple dynasties exchanging their reigns so quickly, the Jews being thrown out and coming back every now and then, the melting pot of the different sects of dynasties and religions—bloody it is a total drag and a drain on your mind!' Sandeep says, all smug while they are coming out after attending their first class on West Asia.

The trio go to the canteen for samosas and coffee. Sandeep is smoking and smiling with satisfaction, happy about making Uday and Mihir pay attention to their MA as well.

'Oh shit! Look, there's Prof. Ali,' Mihir says.

By the time Sandeep and Mihir react, Prof. Ali has already seen them. He knows Sandeep and Mihir since he teaches at KMC.

'Good afternoon, Sir,' they say in a chorus.

'Good afternoon. How are you boys doing?'

'Fine Sir. This is Uday. How come you are here at this hour?' Sandeep says while Uday places an order for coffee and samosas.

'I had a discussion scheduled with Dr Rafique in connection with my thesis. You know I am working on my Ph.D, right?' Prof. Ali answers, sharing Sandeep's cigarette.

'Yes Sir, I remember. It's a very exciting topic—the socio-religious policies during the Mughal regime,' Mihir says, intent on flattering the professor.

'Sir, don't you think that if it wasn't for the fanatic Aurangzeb, the secular and liberal Akbar would not be so hyped up?' Sandeep starts off a debate.

Prof. Ali immediately reacts. 'Liberal and secular Akbar? This is not expected out of you DU lot. I remember you both as mature students of History who respect its interpretative aspect. Sandeep?'

Mihir says, 'Sir, this is the impact of preparing for the civil services. He is training himself for acquiring NCERT eyes on history and is toeing the nationalist view.'

Prof. Ali becomes sad on hearing about the civil services since he had also written the exams thrice. Though a brilliant student, he couldn't make it since he could never score well in CS History. He resumes, 'But I never quit reading History the history way, which is the right way. Getting back to the liberal, secular Akbar. Mihir, argue against it.'

'Sir, he killed Hemu after winning the battle of Panipat, massacred Hindus on a massive scale despite conquering Chittorgarh fort, indulged in gory violence even after the Din-e-ilahi phase to conquer Orissa, Ahmedabad, Kashmir and even Kabul. He was primarily an imperialist out to expand his empire.'

'Yes but why do we confuse all this with secularism? Sandeep, your turn,' Prof. Ali prompts.

'To facilitate his consolidation and expansion he was open to appeasing the native Hindus to bring them into his fold. He abolished Jaziyah, propounded the Din-e-ilahi and Sulh-i-kul in favour of peaceful coexistence,' Sandeep grows passionate. Uday is listening intently, impressing Prof. Ali with his involvement. The coffee is over and the samosas lie untouched.

'Yes, that is where Akbar is different from his predecessors and his successors. Let me tell you, since I am going deep into my research; some very interesting perspectives have been emerging,' Prof. Ali seems prepared for a long discussion. 'In history you can be selective and mine the facts you need. If you want to paint Akbar as secular you can select Din-e-ilahi and the rest and if you want to show him as a hardened imperialist then you select his killings and continued conquests. Nationalist historians needed a model in the medieval times as a reference to prop up secularism and liberalism in the modern times, so the NCERT made Akbar look that way. An ocean of facts will give you multiple visions and truths, so you select only those facts which could prop up the truth you choose. To explain it simply, one can argue both ways, for and against Akbar being secular.' Prof. Ali says, happy to see the boys listening to him in rapt attention.

Uday whispers to Mihir, 'What is the big deal in this revelation? We do this in our daily lives as well.'

Prof. Ali senses that they are getting late. 'I have eaten into much of your CS time but always remember, objectivity in history is utopian. The subject is interpretative and who better to know this than you DU lot? History is history. This history in a particular way is bullshit. But I do hope to meet you guys again. There is nothing like a discourse with bright youngsters beyond the regimen of classes.'

'Bright youngsters? Bullshit! We are so badly screwed. Next Tuesday the fuck spree begins. The first MA paper is "The Rise and Growth of Imperialism",' Uday says glad to be able to talk frankly after Prof. Ali's exit.

'Yes, you're right. We should be hurrying back,' Mihir says.

'Oh man! I left some photocopied notes on my desk in class. They are important. Let's just go up and get them,' Uday says.

'But won't the classrooms be locked by now?' Sandeep says.

'I hope I find somebody.' Uday heads to the class and the other two follow.

Uday finds the doors of the class closed but not locked from outside. He tries opening them but finds that they are locked from the inside. 'Let's go back. We'll check tomorrow morning,' Mihir says.

'Wait man! I can hear some noise. It sounds like somebody is talking in a hushed tone and why should both doors be closed from inside? That proves there is someone inside.'

'Sherlock Holmes! It must be the staff. Just knock and ask for your notes,' Sandeep says.

Uday and Sandeep knock, but no one opens.

'But are we so bothered?' Mihir asks.

'It sounds like English and the voice is a baritone.' Uday is unrelenting. 'Okay, let me look through the window.'

The three find the window closed. Their efforts to peep inside fail. Uday drags an abandoned chair to reach the ventilator but he falls short.

'None of us can reach that high. Enough. We are wasting precious CS time,' Mihir scolds Uday.

'Let me finish. If my hunch is right you won't regret staying back,' Uday says confidently.

Mihir is now curious and heads closer to the window. He hears a female's voice.

'Okay let's try standing on each other's shoulders. I think we can reach the ventilator then,' Sandeep says animatedly.

'But I will be one at the top,' Uday says.

'We have already wasted time. Let me stand here and then Uday can climb on my shoulders.' Sandeep wastes no time in getting into position.

'Wow! What a sight! Gossip isn't always trash and there is never smoke without fire.'

'I'm carrying your weight, so tell us quickly what is happening.' Sandeep sounds annoyed.

'The cowboy Prof. Kumar is with a girl. It's Divya sitting on his thighs. They are kissing. Leave West Asia, Prof. Kapoor is experiencing the entire globe as his hands are all over her body.' Uday is glued to the ventilator.

'If Uday doesn't stop, you should leave and let him remain there doing all those pull-ups hanging from the ventilator,' Mihir says to Sandeep.

Uday gets down and then Sandeep wants to look. Sandeep and Mihir each get a turn before leaving.

'Prof. Kapoor kept going even when my turn came. How was he confident he wouldn't get locked in?' Mihir wonders.

'He must have bribed the staff. What a camouflage! Special classes for special courses. He recently taught about messianic religions and now he is teaching kama after teaching dharma,' Uday says, laughing.

'This is the same Divya whom he has promised a sponsorship to USA for her research,' Sandeep says, turning sombre.

They keep recalling the episode throughout the day. But in the face of their first MA paper, the trio is focused on studying.

'I'm going to Batra. I have to call home. I haven't for almost a week,' Uday says after dinner.

'Okay,' says Mihir.

'Meanwhile, we can also take a stroll to loosen up for another study session,' Sandeep says to Mihir.

'Whenever I study for CS, MA keeps bothering me, and when I pick up the MA notes, I feel guilty. This is what getting screwed means,' Mihir says, trying to crack a joke.

'Don't think about it much. Everyone is in the same boat.'

'But that scene from the afternoon is haunting me. That cowboy is living the life of a casanova.'

The two walk some distance before getting home to see Uday looking a bit sad.

'Is everything all right?' Sandeep asks.

'What happened? When you get upset everyone gets upset,' Mihir tries to cheer Uday up but he is still gloomy.

'It's okay. Don't worry. Just feeling a bit low,' Uday says with a fake smile.

'You were so high before and now you're low. I can smell something fishy,' Sandeep pesters Uday.

'Tell us. There are no secrets between friends,' Mihir pushes.

'I spoke to my mother. Yesterday she went to meet her elder sister for the engagement ceremony of her daughter, my cousin. The entire family was there; all four of her sisters. All my cousins are in the services, IAS, IPS, Revenue, Railways etc. She just told me how her sisters were talking about another bureaucrat being added to the esteemed family since I am trying for the first time this year. She told me how she started boasting about how I would crack the prelims. She is pinning all her hopes on me. After my father left, she managed everything on her own and even started working. Today I feel burdened. I want to get into the civil services for my mother,' Uday explains sombrely.

'Don't worry, it will happen. Just be your happy laughing self. The CS path is already chalked out in your mind, even your second optional is decided and you know quite a bit about it,' Mihir says while Sandeep hugs Uday.

'I am okay. Let me get the notes and figure things out,' Uday smiles as he remembers the scene from earlier in the day. Uday is setting the notes into three piles and seeing him Mihir feels a sense of camaraderie and friendship. He thinks, 'All of us are competing for the civil services yet we are all sharing what we have; our competition is not affecting us. Uday wants it for his mother, Sandeep wants it for his father and for Aparna, and I? For my father, family, society, myself? Sandeep and I are feeling vulnerable seeing Uday worried about CS. Uday is our pace-setter, eternally confident. He has prepared the strategy we are following, apportioning books and arranging notes. He is figuring out the coaching classes and limiting our MA efforts to make sure they don't spill over into CS territory. He contains Sandeep's involuntary drifts towards his MA syllabus and his passionate debates and my tendency for tangential trajectories. He doesn't yield on what he thinks is right and even dictates his desires to his will. He makes no bones even about the Sanjana fling and doesn't hesitate in flaunting his good looks. He radiates the aura of a confident man who is always in control. In contrast, I always tend to doubt my abilities and my efforts. I keep thinking that I should treat this first attempt as testing the waters but at the same time next year reservations would lessen the number of openings but Uday takes everything in his stride. It is this positivity and confidence which win people over.'

~

Krishna Invoked

'God, once this passes it will be a big relief,' Mihir is gripping the notes in his hand and banging them on the desk to show his anger at West Asia. 'It is drab, cluttered and chaotic, an endless sequence of Jews moving from their home, thrown at the mercy of Assyrians, Persians, Babylonians and blah, blah, blah.'

'I am happy about tomorrow. It's the day of deliverance, for now at least, like the deliverance of Jews from Egypt. It's the last paper! Some fun for at least a day or two. The worst thing that could happen is if we have to write this paper again next year,' Uday says.

'But I pity them. They were condemned to permanent exile and they have still not found a peaceful home despite the lofty ideals of democracy, humanism, human rights and peace we keep talking about,' Sandeep adds.

'You two are starting to debate again. I am worried about how to explain this stuff in the answer sheet. It's stuff we never studied even during our graduation,' Uday says.

'I am talking about CS. In the mains GS "Arafat vs Sharon" will occupy a big space in current affairs because the Palestinian conflict is still hot,' Sandeep adds, visibly smug at his ingenuity in discovering a CS camouflage for his history debate.

'Sandy won't rest in peace till he has discharged himself. I can see the Jews itching in his mind. To cut the debate short, they didn't have a powerful King like Constantine to uphold their religion. We just read how Constantine made Christianity a state religion.' Mihir says, his mind getting stirred.

Uday suddenly says, 'You mean their God needed a King to salvage Him out of ignominy.'

'Yes. In fact they did not even have a vigorous apostle like St Paul who could propagate Christianity across Europe,' Sandeep says, happy that Uday is getting drawn into the discussion.

Mihir is noticing Uday smiling on hearing God getting humbled.

'Religious imperialism should be a separate chapter, don't you think?' Mihir asks Uday,

'You're right. It's imperialism. Even the son of God, Jesus, depended on man to win over people to his commandments, which were not too different from the Law of Moses,' Sandeep says.

'We will get back to this when we study Israel vs Palestine. As of now let's focus on tomorrow. We have to go through Sandy's class notes also and there isn't too much time left,' Uday says conclusively.

They are finally through with their MA papers. Sandeep makes an emphatic 'fucked up' gesture at Mihir and Uday while coming out of the classroom.

'Guys I only got two and a half out of four short notes,' Sandeep says angrily.

'Shit. We should have seen last year's questions also. I overheard that there were two questions from last year in this paper. The significance of the messianic religions was not in our notes,' Mihir says, sounding worried.

'But we gave your West Asia more than half a day. I heard that this cowboy Casanova is pretty liberal in evaluating papers. By this time he has already earned a special dividend out of the special classes. That way we may still sail through. Otherwise, repeating next year is always an option,' Uday says optimistically.

'See, here comes Suds the great,' Sandeep says.

'Let's not talk about the paper anymore. What about meeting today evening and getting some beer?' Suds looks like he is in urgent need of sedation.

'Of course. Come over to our place. We have planned some chicken and beer over Sandy's Kishore numbers. Bring Rajan along,' Uday says with his usual cheerful demeanour.

The group goes to the canteen and Uday starts waving at someone.

'I'll be back. You carry on,' Uday moves away.

'Ah! It's Sanjana,' Mihir says.

'He is behaving as if the prelims don't exist. Like a bull unshackled, he can get his deliverance,' Sandeep says mischievously.

'Thinking about Aparna?' Sudhir smiles naughtily at Sandeep.

'No man. A once-in-a-fortnight quota for meetings is fixed.'

'But not all of your meetings are the same. What about that meeting which puts us into exile like the Jews?' Mihir asks mischievously.

'Don't worry, that will come too,' Sandeep says boldly.

Uday and Sanjana join the group.

'This is Sanjana. She is doing her MA in Political Science. She came to the library for some book and wanted to meet you all. These are my friends, Sandeep, Mihir and Sudhir,' Uday makes the introductions.

'Okay. He often talks about you,' Sandeep says to Sanjana.

'Talks of me? Uday? Doesn't seem credible, but...' Sanjana says, smiling shyly at Uday.

'You don't know these types.' Sandeep points at Mihir and Uday. 'I believe egoists are weak; once drawn in, they can't bear their admirers leaving. If you stop feeding their egos, they writhe in misery. As for drawing them into your web of attraction, you just have to shower them with some attention and these lions turn into pussycats.'

'And what about your kind?' Uday counters. 'Don't you like getting attention? Everyone likes it.'

'But my kind isn't blinded by flattery. I am a Buddhist, solid on the ground and someone who takes the middle path. I don't believe in testing others' patience because of my ego, making both myself and the other miserable. I turned the initial attraction into a relationship right away without creating much fuss.'

'Ah! You people are fighting like kids. We are different from each other and that's fine,' Sanjana calms them down.

'No, no! This Buddhist vs autocrat vs communist debate is a normal affair amongst us. This is the beauty of friendship—difference makes it exciting,' Mihir says.

Sudhir says to Sandeep, 'The ego only comes when you have something to flaunt, so from a distance attraction develops only through appearance. Am I right, Bhabhiji?'

Sudhir is searching for the smugness which he knows is in Uday's and Mihir's minds to be reflected on their faces.

The group finishes their coffee and Sanjana gets ready to leave. Uday takes Sanjana to the bus stand for some privacy. He asks his friends to wait for him.

'I wanted to ask you something. You don't look like yourself today. Is something bothering you?' Uday asks Sanjana.

'No, nothing in particular.' Sanjana's words lack conviction.

'Come on, what's wrong? I am not that oblivious,' Uday pesters her.

'My bus is here. Otherwise getting another DTC will be difficult,' Sanjana says. 'I'm glad that I could meet you and your friends. We'll meet up after your prelims. I know you are in the middle of your studies and even I have to study for my JRF (Junior Research Fellowship).'

'Okay, call me and we'll speak.'

She boards the bus and Uday waves at her, then turns away.

'Uday!' he hears her call out. She is standing by the bus that is leaving. Uday looks at Sanjana in amazement and runs towards her.

'I thought I should tell you.'

'Of course. What is the matter?'

'My younger sister has eloped with a boy. He was with her in Hansraj College and they wanted to marry but my father and mother were opposed to it as we are Brahmins from Punjab and the boy is a Mona Punjabi. Things at home are tensed.'

'Aren't you looking for her? Any idea where she might be?'

'Papa says he is not bothered because he is so angry.'

'Caste trouble even in a developed state like Punjab? The

two like each other and that should be enough unless there is some actual issue.'

'I don't like going home anymore. I could share everything with her. Now my home is so stifling with my parents.'

'I agree. No matter how close you are with your parents you can't pour out your heart to them,' Uday says empathetically.

'When I saw you guys together I thought how exciting it would be to live together so freely.'

'Can you wait for a while? They are waiting for me at the canteen. I'll tell them to leave and come back,' Uday asks.

'No, no. Even I have to get back. Mummy will be worried. These days they doubt me as well.'

'But you didn't catch your bus!'

'Don't worry. I will take the DTC from the next stand. I felt like sharing my feelings with you and anyway, saying no to you for anything is beyond me,' Sanjana says with a smile, and though she is blushing her eyes glisten with tears.

A strange but exciting rush of desire, affinity and a sense of authority overtakes Uday. He feels powerful and weak at once; powerful because of what Sanjana said to him and weak because his resolve to stay away from emotional attachment is getting challenged. He looks at Sanjana without saying anything. She says bye and turns away but looks back, her eyes frozen upon him. At this moment they are parting and pairing at the same time.

'Were you setting up your next wild encounter with her or what? We were just coming to get you,' Sandeep says.

For the first time Sandeep's comment doesn't sit well with Uday. He feels an uneasy prick in his heart. Uday is visibly affected but is still trying to overpower his feelings; he loves fighting himself.

'Any emotional issue? You look senti,' Sudhir asks but Uday is in no mood to answer.

In the evening the boys raise a toast with beer to the finale of their MAs. Bahadur has been bribed to stay back longer. Besides Sudhir, Ajit and Alok are present to make the event a festive affair.

'So what were you saying about yourself in the afternoon? You are a Buddhist who follows the middle path? Egotists are weak?' Uday asks Sandeep.

'Yes, of course. Balanced people have reason that helps them tell right from wrong. Egotists get blinded towards reason when someone flatters them.'

'Going by your logic, Krishna was weak. He was an egotist, a true dictator of his desire. He flirted with Radha and enjoyed her attention but got married to Rukmini, not to mention the innumerable gopis. Let me tell you this, Buddhists are boring and when taking the middle path they don't experience the highs that flirtations can give. Winning a girl on your own terms is just fabulous,' Uday retorts.

'But don't you think flirtation should lead to love? That is the key to being peaceful. Krishna probably went through a lot of tension managing both,' Sandeep says smiling at Uday, stretching the Krishna arguement a bit too far.

'No. First let me set the record straight about you calling egotists weak. I chose Krishna whom I consider the most powerful influence on our times. Krishna, on a high after his exciting dalliance with Radha, engineered the biggest-ever battle in human history, the Mahabharata, to establish dharma over adharma. Only an egotist can be that powerful,' Uday says after drinking half a bottle of beer in one go. 'Also, Krishna was a Leo. When is Janmashtami celebrated?' Uday revels in his zodiac association with Krishna.

'History? Mahabharata and Krishna are not history. Not even proto history,' Sandeep says smug at his knowledge of history.

'Update your knowledge. They have discovered the Bet Dwarka and other evidence to prove Krishna was a part of history, making him one of us. Had he been a God I would not even be naming him. Gods don't fascinate me, only man can perform such magnificent feats but man is so humble that he attributes all his good deeds to God,' Uday says, happy to be humbling God again.

'You two have decided to go on and on,' Mihir mediates.

'No no, this is very entertaining. This is a revision of A.L. Basham for us,' Sudhir says while Rajan nods. Rajan is visibly gloomy as he has not been able to make it to the mains, and so is Ajit's roommate Alok.

Uday continues, 'Buddha could not manage even his wife on his path to peace and enlightenment. He was initially planning to end life itself by preaching renunciation; just think if all renounce their married lives and turn celibate, where would we come from? It took him an arduously attained enlightenment to realize this and come back to the world. That is when he preached the middle path. Krishna was wise from the beginning and took both dharma and kama along. Also, don't say that you tread the middle path. Middle means between two things but you are frozen on only one path. Thus, even to prove yourself a Buddhist, you have to flirt with more than one girl.'

Listening to Uday's ingenuous arguments the room resonates with boisterous laughter.

Sandeep does not yield even though he knows Uday can be a pain when rubbed the wrong way. 'Man! You have got it the wrong way. Middle here means a middle path between no desire and extreme desire; so I can safely proclaim that I am a Buddhist, treading the middle path in marrying the girl I love.'

Mihir takes over, sensing that the debate will not end, 'Let me tell you this. Since Uday is so angry at being called weak in front of Sanjana, I will illustrate with an example. In his earlier flat, he picked a fight with his roommate and in a huff walked out. Brijesh, his roommate, making use of the loneliness, indulged himself and sprayed the fluid of desire all over his bed. Uday on returning was infuriated but didn't react. On the following Sunday when Brijesh came back in the afternoon from his Uncle's place, he knocked at the door but nobody opened it in spite of repeated knocking. After a while Uday opened the door, wearing only shorts, to let Brijesh in. Brijesh was left amazed at finding Sanjana in his bed, the bed besmirched mercilessly with the violent sport of desire. So, friends! This is Uday, an ardent fan of Krishna, living the vengeance of Mahabharata in the true sense.'

The assembly breaks into boisterous laughter.

'Right you are, Mihir! Krishna gave the world tested wisdom. The Mahabharata says vengeance is not bad when aimed at a noble end. Had the Mahabharata not taken place and the Pandavas not defeated the Kauravas, the world would have never believed in good. Let me explain. Buddha says "don't lie" whereas Krishna made use of a lie to kill Dronacharya by weakening him emotionally. In the same way deception stands justified if used for a noble end like the deceptive setting of Surya to kill Jayadratha, using cunning to kill Bhishma by planting

Shikhandi before him, etc. Don't you find in your practical life that sometimes for the right reason even lying, deceiving and killing are justified? Just think of a girl who has been raped, killing the perpetrator. Ideals and virtues should be practically pursuable and for man, not God. Thus nothing is absolute, not even values. Buddha's bland noble path, "Right Action, Right Speech, and blah, blah..." don't appeal to me. Krishna any day is more real and, of course, more human than boring Buddha.'

At this moment Sandeep is reminded of the day when they met Prof. Ali, when Uday stated that people somehow tend to discover such facts that could justify their belief, behaviour and action. Knowing Uday, Sandeep's zeal to continue the argument wanes.

The evening proceeds mellifluously with beer, chatting, Sandeep's renditions of Kishore Kumar numbers and mimicking 'Ajit getting into a trance'. And finally everyone disperses after the dinner.

'So just twenty days from now, we will have been through our prelims,' Sudhir sobers the boys down.

For these boys any amount of soma will not douse the fear of CS in their minds.

The party is over and now it's time for them to disperse. They move out, animatedly chatting about CS. The trio finally goes back to their room after bidding adieu to Sudhir, Rajan, Ajit and Alok.

~

The CS Battle Begins

It is the day before the prelims. The trio rummages through all their notes, books, newspapers and magazines. Suddenly they feel as if everything is slipping out of their minds. They realize that it will be impossible to revise everything in a day. They start feeling nervous... That is when they decide to rest before the big day and go for a walk to Batra. But the minds of the three boys have been eclipsed by the single idea of CS and even Batra doesn't seem to calm them down.

'I think when we get back we can quickly brush up on current affairs and nothing beyond that,' Mihir says.

'Yes we must make it a group affair. If we can rope in Ajit it will be wonderful. The fun out of his company would help us escape our own minds,' Uday says to lighten the mood.

'In fact let's go back via Ajit's place and that way we can pick him along,' Sandeep says.

'That is a wonderful idea,' Mihir agrees, but not without the thought of empathy at the back of his mind.

Ajit and Alok have been persuaded out of their CS

hibernation. No matter how intense or expansive the misery, the mind has a penchant for recovery.

'Who was the winner of the Men's US Open tennis match this year?' Uday asks Ajit.

'Wait a minute. I definitely know this.' Ajit immediately disappears into his usual trance and the rest exchange glances and mimic him as always. They have tea and after waiting for a few minutes Ajit comes out of his trance. They get the better of their nervous anxiety.

Mihir, Uday and Sandeep go to bed earlier than usual but struggle to fall asleep. Through the night, Mihir and Uday ask each other twice whether it is time to wake up while Sandeep manages to sleep. It is a night of multiple dawns.

'Haaaah....!' Mihir sighs contentedly.

'I think it was okay,' Sandeep says happily.

'We will manage to...' Uday says with a nod.

'They did say some questions would be unexpected but we can still check for our score in the evening. I wish I could fly home, I feel so totally drained,' Uday says with a sense of relief.

'Here you won't get the soma to afford your flight,' Sandeep says.

'I think we deserve to take an auto. I don't feel like taking a bus,' Mihir says.

All the MN boys reach the designated flat to find out their final scores. The event is like an excavation but goes as deep as a standard fifth NCERT history book. Getting something wrong is like doing it all wrong. Getting a doubtful right answer is like getting closer to God and a confirmation of answers known for sure gives a sense of elation. The trio emerges triumphant after some marathon mulling.

'Shit man, I thought I would sleep like a log but I can't seem to fall asleep,' Uday says after struggling for almost an hour.

Mihir answers from the other room, 'Excitement isn't letting us sleep. It happens even when one is extremely happy.'

Even Sandeep joins in, 'We should drink enough to be able to pass out.'

'That is for tomorrow. We'll go to my old place, Brijesh's, if you want to really fly with soma; he is the right man.' Uday has already planned it out.

'But you don't live with him anymore,' Sandeep says.

'Yeah. But childhood chemistry never stops working and Brijesh grabs any opportunity to booze. He can afford a lavish party, so tomorrow it will be in his house,' Uday replies.

'That means there will be no hassle in organizing the affair. That's really great and his cook makes great snacks,' Mihir says.

The next day is restful. The trio decides to only enrol themselves in Abhash Singh's GS classes and not talk about CS any further. Uday has made sure of their acceptance and only the formalities need to be completed. He says, 'Brijesh is content, doesn't nurture any specific ambitions, fully participates in another's happiness, lavishly feeds everyone with compliments and will make sure the evening is fun. He is skilled in fostering fun with booze and bonhomie.' Mihir thinks, 'My knowledge of the human species is very limited. I didn't know that humans who instantly turn benevolent for booze also exist.'

'So you are sure to crack CS in the first go?' a tipsy Brijesh asks as he pours a third glass of beer.

'Two glasses of beer are not enough to beguile me. The prelims are not even half a ride,' Uday replies to Brijesh.

'That means prelims will need gallons of beer to rise to the head,' Sandeep says, drinking his beer bottoms up and looking for a refill.

'Yes, small successes need bathing in soma to weave up a high,' Mihir says and finishes his drink.

'Small? Ask those who didn't make it. The first step is not small. Ironically, the foundation stone is fated to face this ignominy but...' Brijesh counters Mihir's philosophy with his own philosophy.

Uday had described Brijesh as a party animal. He knows a little of everything—like poetry, both English and Urdu; music, from jazz to ghazals; and even dance, from salsa to street. He even keeps up with current affairs to work with the intelligent crowd. So Brijesh has brewed his personality to ensure copious draughts of soma. He is extroverted and confident, and fluent in Hindi, Urdu and English. But these qualities have only given him an exaggerated perception of his own self and he goes overboard to impress people around him. The interactions between Uday and Brijesh are always fun to watch because it's a duel of élan.

So the party continues late into the night. The dinner pales when everyone is intoxicated under the towering influence of the sublime soma. Finally calling it a night, the trio staggers out.

'Let me tell you frankly, I deliberately withheld my piss to enjoy this sense of liberation. There is nothing to beat pissing beer out on this high. If this is the feeling from having beer, I wonder what the Gods enjoyed when they had ancient soma,' Uday says.

'Why do you bring God into the picture? I feel like you are obsessed with God,' Sandeep says.

'That is why God sits in perpetual hibernation. He knows

even non-believers remember Him with equal fervour. You either hate Him or love Him but you can't remain indifferent to him,' Mihir joins in.

'That means God has fun. It is amazing how masochistic man can be. He created God to rule over himself,' Uday has the last word.

The next day Sandeep announces, 'You two are going for an afternoon movie show today. Your Bhabhi is visiting.' He always lets everyone know at the last minute because he feels his plans might change. When it comes to Aparna, Sandeep lives with a philosophy that tomorrow is far away and today is all one has. Also, telling them the news in that very morning reduces the amount of time he has to face embarrassment and guilt in chasing out Mihir and Uday. At times Mihir and Uday even have to watch some B-grade movies to pass the time. But the sense of sacrifice being made for their friend makes the exile enjoyable. 'Celebrating the prelims? The results aren't out yet. But I must commend your precision. Prelims done and Bhabhiji in,' Uday says playfully.

'There is no movie worth watching today,' Mihir says, trying to make Sandeep feel guiltier.

'You two are ruthless opportunists. Okay, embarrass me as much as you want. I will wait for my turn,' Sandeep turns strategically emotional. Turning to Mihir he continues, '*Khiladi* is playing at Batra and just the other day you were telling me you like the song "*Wada raha sanam, honge juda na hum, chahe na chahe zamana*" because the singer reminded you of Kishore Kumar.'

'Well said! You want us to sing that for your love story. Let's call his elder brother and uncle from Ranchi. They will be the perfect audience to this song throwing them a challenge on

Sandy's behalf.' Uday laughs, happy to make fun of Sandeep.

'Just you wait till Sanjana arrives,' Sandeep says.

'She is getting here early today. We are together for a long day.' Uday dangles the keys of Brijesh's room right in Sandeep's face. Whenever Brijesh is out, he gives his keys to Uday so that he can enjoy his amorous encounters with Sanjana.

'Fuck you. He is too smart for us,' Sandeep tells Mihir. 'But what about you, Mihir?'

'No issues, I will manage with Suds. I have anyway been missing his discourses on harrowed Harries,' Mihir says but not without a pang in his heart.

'Ah! I never knew you would also be "occupied" today,' Uday says to Sandeep with a sense of guilt at leaving Mihir alone.

Everything is fixed. Sandeep will meet Aparna in his flat, Uday will meet Sanjana in Brijesh's flat and Mihir will spend time with Sudhir. Sandeep is in the kitchen getting some special food prepared and Uday is in the bathroom. Mihir is sitting on the bed reading the newspaper and thinking, 'In the sinful and frenzied encounter of the duo captivated in the throes of passion, this bed will be devoured by desire.' As he is thinking, a picture of Bhabhi enters his mind. A journey of this sort once begun in the mind never ends. It meanders to different tracks with ease without causing even a jerk in his train of thoughts. Different pictures flash in his mind: Uday with Sanjana, Mukesh with his landlady, an Afghan lady ogling at Mihir during his evening Batra stroll and finally Jyoti. 'Alas! If I could just make up my mind and respond to Jyoti to get into the league of Uday and Sandeep, balancing dharma and desire. But what if I get lost in the labyrinth of lust or the deluge of emotion?'

Mihir is the last one to leave after Bahadur and Uday. He

has locked the door from the front, leaving Sandeep and Aparna in their cosy den. He throws the keys inside, flinging them through the window.

He reaches Sudhir's to find him and Rajesh in the hall.

'Hi Suds! Hi Rajan!'

'Hey Mihir. We were just thinking of you all. Where are Sandeep and Uday?' Sudhir asks.

Mihir just smiles mysteriously and Sudhir instantly understands.

'Bhabhiji?' Sudhir asks.

'You're feeling relieved after prelims, I guess. What about mains?' Mihir directs his question at Rajesh for some tips even though the latter has not been able to make it.

'I have decided on Geography for my second optional. How about you?' Sudhir asks Mihir.

'I am going for Anthropology and so is Sandeep. Uday has already decided on Pub. Ad. and is definitely better placed than us,' Mihir replies. He seems eager about mains and is full of doubts about how to make it through and how to manage the two optionals and everything else.

'We have not talked about CS for a day and it seems as if it has been ages,' Sudhir says.

'You people are on the right track. This is how alcoholics feel when they don't drink for an evening. That is the way to win CS,' Rajan says.

Mihir turns to Rajan, 'For the optional, how do I decide what to study from the pool of materials?'

'You will not find too many differences amongst them so just focus on properly remembering what you study,' Rajan counsels. Mihir is still full of doubt, thinking that the coaching institutes and their study material can't be the keys to succeeding in the civil services.

Rajan senses how Mihir feels since he'd felt the same way when he was preparing for his mains last year.

'How are you improving this year? Have you thought about why you didn't make it last year?' Mihir asks Rajan.

Rajesh replies, 'There is no limit to improving when you have to remember such a vast syllabus by rote. One can go on adding to knowledge, modifying notes, practising question papers, etc. What about the person who cracks it in the first shot? Going by that logic someone writing mains for the third or fourth time will automatically be more solid in his knowledge and practice. The world of CS is mesmerizing and I can give you multiple examples to prove how weirdly it behaves.'

'So he says just stay afloat and don't try to discover a formula since there exists none. Do you know Sudhanshu from Hindu? He was the topper in History, quite senior to us. He didn't get through mains even though he wrote the exam four times. Then there was Rajeev Verma, whom you know. And there's Rohit Singh. He couldn't even get through prelims and we thought given a chance he would crack mains in the first go. One of my Hatian seniors got through mains but finally couldn't make it. And the last one—in the flat next to ours there is a graduate in Hindi from Darbhanga University, who even sings in Hindi and Maithili, who struggles with basic English. He came in last year and cracked CS right in the first attempt with the 237th rank. He wrote History in Hindi medium and Sanskrit, scored 375 in Sanskrit, more than making up for his 80 in the interview,' Sudhir says to calm Mihir down.

'You're forgetting that boy from Gaya. Under the influence

of Buddhism, he attained enlightenment that the language of Pali would give him his salvation in CS. He wrote the exams in Pali and shot through into the IAS right in his first attempt,' Rajan says.

'And then that biker who we saw at Batra the same day we saw the Pandit?' Sudhir asks, laughing at the memory of his assessment of the man.

'Just a while back you mentioned that Sanskrit chap from Darbhanga scripting a thrilling success story, so why are you making fun of the Pandit?' Mihir asks, to emphasize that appearances can be deceptive.

The boys have some tea and snacks. Mihir looks at his watch since he can go back to the flat by 2.30 p.m. They have lunch and then Mihir heads home.

Mihir is surprised to find the door still locked when he reaches. He thought Sandeep would have unlocked the front door after Aparna left. Sensing Mihir's presence, Sandeep peeps out to tell him, 'Just go somewhere nearby and come back after half an hour.' Before Mihir can ask any questions he says, 'Please don't ask any questions. I will explain later,' Sandeep sounds nervous.

Mihir wanders around aimlessly and meets Uday returning after his date. 'Why are you loitering outside at this hour?' Uday asks Mihir.

'I have no idea what the issue is. Sandeep was worried and asked me to stay out. Let's go and check what the matter is,' Mihir explains.

Hearing their footsteps, Sandeep hands them the key and they open the door. They enter to find Aparna leaving in a hurry. Uday and Mihir are intensely curious.

Uday asks, 'For God's sake, tell us something instead of

standing there gulping down water.'

'Hold up. Let me settle down and get my breath back,' Sandeep falls onto the bed. 'It was about 1 p.m. and Aparna and I were in the kitchen getting some food. Then I felt like I was hearing Bhaiya's voice and got really nervous but I thought I was imagining it. Then I heard the voice again and my heart started beating faster. I shifted my attention to the back door in no time. I heard him near the back door since he must have tried the front one first before going around the back. He was talking to somebody, "Has Sandeep gone out?"

"Yeah, I think all of them are out," I recognized Ajit's voice.

'I instantly regretted telling my family about studying with those guys because otherwise Bhaiya would not have checked with them.

'"Should I go back or wait for a while?" Bhaiya asked.

'"Did Sandeep know you were coming?" Ajit asked.

'"No he doesn't. I was actually escorting my schoolboys on a trip to Mussoorie and Delhi is where we're stopping before heading on. We're taking the night train and I didn't think I would have the time to meet him so I didn't tell him," Bhaiya replied. That's when I thought he had kept me in the dark on purpose and had just come to spy on me.

'"Since you have come all this way, come and wait at my place and have some tea. I will keep the back door open so that we can hear them once they come back," Ajit offered.

'In my head I was cursing Ajit. I was just waiting for you guys to come. Aparna couldn't have left from the back door because of Bhaiya being right there. I could not have asked Sonu either. That's why when Mihir came I asked him to go back because I was scared Bhaiya might come out at that moment.

I had already heard him saying to Ajit, "I think I should leave now." Fear teaches one every skill so even after Bhaiya left I waited to be sure. That's when you guys arrived. Now I realize that while anyone can be courageous in their head, translating that to real life is a different ballgame altogether.'

Uday laughs hysterically.

'You have a black tongue. You're the one who wished this morning that Bhaiya would come,' Sandeep says, half angry and half amused.

'If that's the case then we are definitely getting into the IAS, since I have said it. Anyway, I am really hungry. Let's eat if there is anything left.'

'Go ahead and eat. We didn't eat anything,' Sandeep says.

'You two eat. I ate at Sudhir's,' Mihir says.

'Why didn't you eat? You got the paneer made specially for Bhabhiji and you let her go hungry?' Uday asks sarcastically.

'You can't eat when you are fighting for your survival.'

'But I hope you had your screw before the horror show started.' Uday and Mihir laugh.

'What happened, my dear balanced Buddhist? Is the middle path between your love and your family so tough?'

'Ah let him be, he is already so tensed,' Mihir says sympathetically.

'Some twain can never meet and sometimes middle path is not feasible,' a deflated Sandeep says.

'That's why Krishna abducted his own wife, Rukmini, and got even his sister, Subhadra, abducted so she could marry Arjuna. Some decisions can't be taken with a consensus; convincing everyone at the same time is just not feasible. Krishna was wise enough to know this from the beginning,' Mihir explains.

West Asia and Prelims Success

The boys have begun preparing for the mains. The trio has opted for evening sessions of GS coaching. Uday appears set with his choices of History and Pub. Ad. He has decided he will not look beyond what he has already and his notes are tried and tested since they already helped his elder cousin enter the services. Mihir and Sandeep are struggling with Anthropology. They are compiling notes out of some university tutorials, Bajirao and some standard textbooks, a time-consuming and exasperating affair. They have divided the job with Mihir working in the library and Sandeep at home. Mihir remains doubt-ridden despite counselling from different corners, while Sandeep continues to be stirred out of the CS rhythm by the MA results and his JRF preparation.

'Shit! We forgot to check our results. They were supposed to be out yesterday,' Sandeep says to Uday, waking up Mihir.

'That shows you are on the right track,' Uday says with no excitement.

'Mihir, are you coming?' Sandeep gets ready to leave and

Mihir stays in bed. Uday and Mihir listen to Sandeep rush through his chores.

'I hope you two come along. Anyway, we have to check the results today or tomorrow.'

'Okay, man. Mihir, come on, otherwise Sandy will go mad alone.'

'Fine, let's check how West Asia has screwed us,' Mihir says.

They leave and reach the university.

'You have fooled us so well!' Sandeep screams at Mihir after reading the results on the notice board.

'What do you mean?' Mihir asks and even Uday looks confused.

'55 in West Asia? Mihir, you have really ditched us,' Sandeep says with genuine anguish. Sandeep had felt MA was his forte.

'Mihir, not fair!' Uday, though indifferent, joins in to support Sandeep.

'But what about Sandy scoring the highest overall?' Mihir tries to divert their attention from himself.

'You take care of yours. Sandy's was expected,' Uday retorts.

'But even I am surprised. Sandeep has probably read it wrong,' Mihir moves towards the notice board and Uday follows.

'Look at your scores! They exceed 55 overall. Mihir and I are true friends, stuck around the 52 mark,' Uday says to Sandeep.

'I am really perplexed. Believe me,' Mihir says.

'You are cheating on us. Come on, tell me your secrets,' Uday jokes in a friendly manner.

'I can't take it anymore. Listen to me,' Mihir is visibly tensed.

'Come on Sandeep, let us hear him out. The play begins. Now Mihir, tell us what you have to say. Is the act of library study beyond us?' Uday says.

'I hope he doesn't come up with some cock-and-bull story. I know he isn't that kind but I am curious to know what he did for the evaluator to belch out a 55,' Sandeep says.

'I had written only two-and-a-half crammed answers and the rest was just crisis management; inventing logic out of infinity and twisting it to fit the question. Everyone does it but I guess the examiner liked the way I did it,' Mihir explains.

Sandeep is far from convinced. 'Let me be specific. Tell me what you wrote for the influence of ancient West Asia in the sphere of religion. You said that that was the unprepared one you attempted.'

Mihir begins, 'Okay. "West Asia in ancient times was a melting pot seething with violence and destruction due to protracted warfare amongst several dynasties vying for power and influence over the region extending from Turkey and Israel in the west to Persia and Afghanistan in the East. Power shifted between several dynasties including the Assyrians, Babylonians, Byzantinians, Persians etc. and later the Islamic dynasties like the Umayyads and Abbasids. The people were sick of violence without any hope.

'"Out of this melting pot emerged the messianic religions Judaism, Christianity and Islam. When man did not listen to man about the futility of violence and destruction, supernatural sanction had to be invoked to impress moral order upon them. Hence emerged the idea of the messiah, or messenger of God, who conveys His message of peace to the people. These messiahs were Abraham and Moses for Judaism, Jesus Christ for Christianity and Prophet Mohammed for Islam. They gave people the belief that God wants peace and fraternity in his kingdom.

'I summed it up like this, "These messianic religions

emerged out of a human need for peace and happiness. Secondly, they emphasized upon the unity and oneness of God. Thirdly, these religions went a long way in aligning religions with morality." In my answer, while expressing the utilitarian view of religion I could not resist the temptation to express my doubt about the reality of these messiahs being divine messengers of God. I explained that while there is evidence of the birth and crucifixion of Jesus Christ, I know of no conclusive evidence of his transfiguration, resurrection and ascension to heaven. Nor do I know that of the transfiguration of Abraham at Mt Sinai. These may have been conceived by man to give divine sanction to his own objectives of sanity and purpose.'

'Damn. He has explained it really well,' Sandeep is visibly impressed.

'The examiner must have been either agnostic or atheist which is why he came under the spell of the answer,' Uday says.

Sandeep tells Uday about an incident that occurred when they were doing their graduation, when Mihir got into trouble tackling the Medieval India paper, having prepared for only questions and still managed to score 58. 'I can still recall the time he had written some long spiel about Noorjahan. The question was "Describe the significance of Noorjahan's reign in medieval India." We had left out the Begum as the question had appeared in last year's paper as well. Then Mihir went off on a tangent and wrote something about Noorjahan, Islam and gender bias. He said he had written only one big paragraph, "During Jahangir's reign, it was actually Noorjahan who controlled the affairs of the state. After Jahangir's death she wove a plot for the succession of Shahryar, Jahangir's weaker son, instead of Shah Jahan, so that she could continue wielding her influence. Islam says that women are inferior to men and thus should be subservient to them. However, the example of Noorjahan dominating the Mughals for such a long time and nearly outsmarting Shahjahan belies this notion of women being weak. Noorjahan along with Raziya Begum during the time of the Sultanate goes down in medieval Indian history as an example challenging this fallacy of women being inferior to men.'

'Going by these examples, it looks like Mihir should deliberately not study some important CS topics and leave them to the mercy of his mind,' Uday says.

Sandeep agrees, 'This shows that necessity is the mother of invention and creativity is a function of crisis.'

'Not only that, invention is always appreciated, that too when one makes such heady cocktails,' Uday concludes.

They get into a routine again of preparing for the mains. However, with the prelims results still awaited a sense of unease becomes the background music of their lives.

One evening Mihir, Uday and Sandeep are at Batra, drinking juice after their GS classes. The peace is broken by a sudden noise. They hear the vroom of many mobikes building into a razzmatazz. The excited riders are seen speeding away under some spell. The excitement is then deciphered to mean that the prelims results are out. It's what happens at Batra whenever any UPSC results come out. The bikers collected the roll numbers of many people to find out as many results as they can and they never refuse anyone. In the CS world there is no discrimination amongst the worshippers.

For the rest left behind waiting it is a hollowed existence; only butterflies in the stomach and pounding hearts exist in an inextricable messy mix to leave the hosts in misery. The sensory world ceases to exist. At this moment, no soma can sedate these hapless boys. Optimism goes for a toss, their minds haunted by all the wrong answers in their answer sheets, their anxiety amplifying their irrational fears.

The first group gets back with only two successful candidates and the trio's fear deepens. The bikers are empathetic and benevolent; they convey the positive results by triumphantly gesticulating from afar in order to calm down the tumult in the aspirants and a no is revealed with a deflated whimper. The second caravan screeches to a stop, announcing six out of ten. Among those six are Sandeep, Uday and Mihir.

They instantly hug each other in happiness, controlling their emotion in front of a sad Ajit who has not made it.

'I think we should let our families know,' Uday says.

'Yes, we should,' Mihir says.

'I hope Bhaiya is not home, otherwise he will write it off saying it's only the prelims, snatching away my happiness,' Sandeep says as the three head to the STD booth.

'This chap is definitely talking to his girlfriend,' Uday says impatiently about the person inside the booth. After waiting some more, Sandeep goes up to the person inside and gestures him to quickly come out.

The three of them plan a celebration which includes beer, chicken and vintage Bachchan.

'I actually felt a little guilty when telling my mum the prelims results. She is so happy. If I don't make it through mains she will…' Uday says seriously.

'Same here. Papa was elated and ignored the fact that I am only experimenting. Their expectations won't come down,' Mihir also feels the same way.

'The story is completely different in my case. Bhaiya wrote it off saying it's only the result for the prelims. Papa threw a gauntlet and said I have to justify being in Delhi,' Sandeep says thinking 'If only my family could also enjoy the small achievements!'

The three are drinking and chatting. Mihir talks about his fears of being happy in the face of the impending mains, still doubting his efforts. Uday assures everyone that everything is under control. Sandeep, serious about his MA, feels happy that his CS deficit will be made up by Uday's organization.

'But Ajit was sad, more so since the rest of the group got through,' Mihir says.

'Efforts or no efforts, results tend to make you feel sad,' Sandeep says.

'Don't worry, Mihir. We will conquer CS,' Uday says brimming with enthusiasm.

'But I am not expecting a miracle,' Mihir sounds sceptical.

'In this world these are the only miracles that happen,' Alok says as he walks into the apartment with Ajit. 'When it is CS, anything is possible.'

Mihir thinks, 'Alok is just one amongst many who say that.'

'Ajit! Don't feel sad. Didn't you listen to your friend? Even I know people who failed thrice failed in the prelims and then directly got into the IAS in their fourth attempt,' Sandeep says.

'It's fine. I was not expecting it anyway,' Ajit replies.

As they watch Bachchan movies, their high shoots up, a mixture of soma, Bachchan and CS. Uday is drinking more than the rest. He has a penchant for going overboard, particularly when watching Bachchan. They have the chicken that Bahadur serves under the haze of the movie.

'Oh mere dil ke chain, chain aaye mere dil ko dua kijiye,' Sandy starts singing Kishore Kumar as they wait for dinner. Uday is extremely drunk. Suddenly he shouts, 'Sandy, where is the chain you sing of, I mean solace' and throws up.

'Shit, hurry up with the water.' Sandeep tries to hoist Uday up but he is already drooling on the bed. Mihir goes for the water while Ajit tries to wipe up the vomit.

'Make him lie down and he'll feel better.' Mihir forces Uday to drink some lime water. At that moment he is reminded of the day Uday served him lemonade when he felt sick, Mona Lisa rising in his mind again.

'Sorry!' Uday says guiltily.

Sandeep doesn't forget his duel even while attending to Uday. 'That's why I always tell you that Buddha's middle path is the best.'

'Actually it is God's turn to be angry with him. He has chosen him to display the side effects of soma.' Mihir tries to lighten the atmosphere.

'You two are taking advantage of Uday's sickness. Don't provoke him otherwise he'll show the viraat roop of Krishna,' Alok says.

The boys finish eating and switch off the movie. As Ajit and Alok leave Alok remarks, 'In the dark he probably drank too much.' Uday has fallen asleep without eating. Mihir goes to bed but his mind is buzzing. 'In our friendship, human virtues of sharing and caring don't entail any mental and physical costs. It is effortless and devoid of discomfort.'

The trio are going great guns at their mains. Life has again settled into a routine.

~

The Mystique of Desire

We think of destiny as being predetermined. But do we keep believing in destiny without ever doubting it? The thing is, despite doubt destiny keeps conveying strong hints of its existence.

It had been two weeks since Mihir had seen Jyoti. He had already sunk into a state where not seeing Jyoti in the library made his day feel empty. The feeling of something missing fluctuated through the day and the intensity of it depended on the extent to which his CS preparations could absorb him.

'Hey! How are you finding your library sessions these days?' Sandeep asks. He has met Mihir at the tea stall.

'They are okay but the mains are driving me crazy. It's too much to remember by rote in three months.' Mihir knows he is not answering Sandeep's intended query.

'I mean, aren't you missing someone in the library?' Sandeep smiles mischievously.

'Not again! I know you're talking about Jyoti.' Mihir concentrates on his tea to avoid Sandeep's mischievous gaze.

'But wait. No one can deny that you know her and even you can't deny that you know her well. On occasions like this one even strangers feel sympathetic towards the bereaved, and you...' Sandeep says with a mixture of sombreness and mischief.

'What do you mean?' Mihir says impatiently.

'She lost her father. That Football told me just a while back,' Sandeep was referring to Navin, a short stocky boy, who always offers his services to girls for whatever help they might need. Football's passport to popularity is his physique and his insatiable urge to be in the company of girls. They use him like an errand boy, getting him to arrange notes, bring coffee and accompany them to movies and restaurants. His compensation is the feeling of importance, by way of his physical proximity to girls. 'You are Kishan Kanhaiya,' the boys always make fun of him. Sandeep often says, 'How can one be so illiterate in reading expressions? Just look at that duffer! He is bursting with pride and he can't see that the boys are making fun of him. Bloody he spices up even a simple handshake with girls, making it seem like amorous hand-holding. It's like his desperation for the company of girls has drugged him.'

Sandeep tries to gauge Mihir's feelings by the amount of concern on his face. Mihir's concern at the news of Jyoti's father's death would show how much he is tied to Jyoti.

'That is definitely reason enough to feel sad. Everyone deserves sympathy.' Mihir rationalizes his sadness.

'But your face tells a different story. What is the point of pushing her out of your brain? Some things should be allowed to develop naturally. Some control definitely brings order, but too much of it is nothing but a means to stir anarchy. You are a History guy; don't be a communist to yourself; allow your other emotions in. Why are you scared? You are fiercely focused on your CS and you can balance your desire with your ambition. There is a very thin line between conflict and chaos; don't be an extremist and come on to the middle path of Buddha. It is the weak who rebel against their emotions; the strong revel in the challenge of reconciling conflicting emotions.'

Mihir is still sceptical but he does seem to be coming around to what Sandeep is saying.

They finish their tea.

'You are the best judge but I think you should meet her at least. She is more than a classmate to you,' Sandeep says as he walks away.

Mihir is heading back to the library but he suddenly stops and heads to the PG classroom. He knows Football will be there with the girls for the post-class gossip. He gets to the first floor and sees Football with three girls.

'Hello!' Rashmi screams, one of few people in the class acquainted with Mihir.

'Hi,' Football says, turning to acknowledge Mihir's arrival. He does not like any extra male presence in the group. The niceties exchanged between any of his girls with anyone else, especially Mihir, makes him feel insecure. But Jyoti has somehow transcended Football's possessiveness to connect with Mihir in her silent way, and even Football knows that.

'Hey! Seeing you after a long time. I think we met last in the West Asia class,' Rashmi says.

'Hey! You know, Jyoti lost her father about a week back,' Football says to Mihir, showing off his knowledge of Jyoti's life.

'Yes, it's pretty sad,' Rashmi says. 'We went to her place last Saturday.'

The sudden mention of Jyoti has to do more with the Jyoti–Mihir saga than the sadness of bereavement.

'Did you meet her?' Football asks Mihir, his concern coming from the pleasure of knowing that Mihir never broke the ice with Jyoti.

'No, I didn't see her in the library but I didn't know this was the reason,' Mihir says, relieved that he didn't have to push for details.

'You must pay her a visit. Now it's only her, her mother and elder sister. Everyone who knows her have visited her place. I thought you also...' Rashmi says.

'How is everything else? I mean the classes and everything? Are the professors still shooting CS absentees with their aggressive sarcastic remarks?' Mihir tries to change the subject.

'Prof. Shukla never misses an opportunity to pass a remark about CS,' Rashmi says.

'Then what else do we do? Keep groping in the blind alley of ad hoc appointments, having to earn each year the lease of one year of work? And that too when one has finally succeeded in clearing the NET or JRF? Besides, everyone knows how difficult it is to manage a guide for the Ph.D. They don't want the best coming into academics. There aren't enough colleges to absorb them either,' Mihir says.

'That is true. Everyone knows what it takes to discover a guide; sycophancy, a personal equation and... Let it go. The lesser said the better,' Rashmi says aggressively.

'It's a huge psychological drain. Students like Rohit Singh are still struggling,' Mihir says passionately. 'And just think about those who don't get even the ad hoc tag. It is never a fight to the finish. They keep trying every year and get pushed onto the cliff after the five-year time limit of the JRF is exhausted. They have ensured that it remains the refuge of the CS flounders.'

Football interrupts Mihir, 'Mihir is now in his natural element, talking philosophy.'

'But he is right. Our value system is flawed,' Rashmi says.

One of the girls points to her watch to signal how late it is.

'Okay. It's time for my last bus,' Rashmi says.

Mihir goes back to the library, gripped with the thought of how to overcome his mental battle about going to meet Jyoti. He thinks how easy it would have been if he was just a classmate but their silent attraction complicates matters. He packs up and leaves for the Patel Chest bus stand. He is thinking of how to express his condolences; however, the idea of being with her is greater in his mind. He knows that if his confusion dominates his human sensitivity he will feel very guilty.

His inner sensitivity precipitates a decision; he will go to meet Jyoti on Saturday. Having made the decision, he remains in the same thought process. 'Silence has such a power of communication. Can it be so unequivocal? Jyoti and I barely spoke to each other but the world knows the chemistry between us. Destiny has willed me to finally break the ice with her. It's ironical that it took an adversity, the death of Jyoti's father, to make me focus on the chemistry we have. Calling it love would be jumping the gun. It is nothing but destiny. Man keeps doubting it despite being witness to its play. But this bizarre restlessness throbbing within me is a mix of guilt and thrill, the guilt of finally taking the path of desire I had pledged not to and the thrill of finally getting to communicate with Jyoti. It probably happens to everyone but they manage to live cosily with their conflicting emotions. Anyway, destiny has a penchant for doing Mona Lisa to me. But I will not rue my guilt; it is a symptom of my resolve to remain focused on my ambition. For quite some time now thoughts of her have been captivating me, especially at night in bed when darkness illuminates desire. Am I on Sandeep's middle path? Or will my encounter with Jyoti end only at Uday's dabbling with desire without getting into senti hanky-panky?'

Mihir wakes up on Saturday morning feeling sort of possessed. He finishes his chores, gets ready and leaves for Jyoti's house all in a trance. His heart is in a hurry to see Jyoti but something delays his steps on the stairs.

'Ah! Hello,' Jyoti says as she opens the door. Her expressions convey an instant familiarity. She looks behind him to see if he has come alone.

'No one else. I have come alone,' Mihir says. She is surprised because she expected him to come with someone to overcome his shyness.

'I actually found out what happened just a few days back,' Mihir says as he walks into the house.

Mihir notices that his presence brings a certain calm on Jyoti's face. He also notices her puffy eyes that speak of a lot of crying. She looks sad and tired of being sad too. No matter how big the tragedy is, life needs to go on. How much of life the living has is a different matter.

'Let me get you some water,' Jyoti says, guiding Mihir to the living room.

Mihir is pained at seeing Jyoti completely drained of her springiness. His eyes fall upon a garlanded picture of her father on the wall. The frame makes the void enveloping the house all the more poignant. It is so vivid that it appears as if it is talking to the beholder. The absence of a person lends speech and expression to his picture.

'I hope I haven't disturbed you,' Mihir says, taking the offered water. He can't help being uncomfortably shy.

'No, not at all. I didn't expect you even though many others from class have already paid their customary visits,' Jyoti says with a slight spark in her eyes. Mihir draws contentment from her 'your-visit-is-not-customary' expression.

Mihir and Jyoti sit together is an uneasy togetherness. Tackling a stranger is easier than tackling a familiar stranger. They both know each other but somehow don't know each other. They know how they smile, how they walk, how they sit, how they dress up. The only thing left is to actually talk to each other, which will help them know more about one another.

Jyoti is flustered. Her first meeting with the muse of her desire is happening under the shadow of her father's death. Destiny has tricked her also into a Mona Lisa.

'Is there no one else in the house?' Mihir asks.

'No, Mummy and Didi have gone to Haridwar to consign the ashes to the Ganga,' Jyoti says, immediately reminded of her grief. Her eyes well up as she says the word 'ashes'; it was as if they were just waiting for a push to spill over.

'I am sorry. I don't believe in a surfeit of condolences because they disturb the dynamics of grief and pain. Whether people come or not, grief only diminishes with time and sometimes their presence makes the pain worse. Being alone is important to recover. See how I have made you cry again,' Mihir says guiltily.

At this moment Mihir thinks, 'Man is designed such that no emotion lasts very long.'

'No no. Not all arrivals are distant,' Jyoti says, reassuring

Mihir that his presence is not untimely.

'Okay I won't ask you any more questions. You share whatever you want with me. I am listening.' Mihir looks at the picture on the wall. It is too prominent to be missed. Jyoti's eyes follow Mihir's gaze and again fill with tears.

'A living man lies frozen in a frame. They rightly say that prana escapes from the body to merge into the void,' Jyoti gestures at the space around her. 'If that is the case, no matter how infinite the void is, he probably is here as well.'

'You are right. There is no other way to describe atma or prana, whatever you may call it. Actually, the word "balloon" comes to mind when I try to describe life. It bursts and the air escapes into nothingness while the membrane or the body lies lifelessly on the ground to be consigned to the earth. Thus the void suggests Brahma and the earth, body. I do agree that philosophy is the reasoning of the uncertain and the unknown and it serves a practical purpose by providing a much-needed anchor to the human mind in such distress.' Mihir says sombrely. *Life* anyway is his favourite muse.

'They say after death the soul merges into Brahma and attains Paramananda. Then why does this final act involve so much pain? The one who attains it is also filled with fear and those left behind are left in tears,' Jyoti responds, sombreness sinking deeper into her eyes and taming her tears.

Mihir is uncomfortable, confused whether he should go to Jyoti and calm her down or keep sitting there and wait for the grief to complete its passage through her heart. In view of their chemistry, he is shy about being in close physical proximity with her and them being alone in the house enhances his discomfiture. Jyoti suddenly realizes Mihir's presence and she wipes her tears to try and get back to normal.

Mihir thinks, 'It is strange how one can cry so much. Tear glands are a part of the human anatomy because God knew that man would need them to manage grief and pain. It is all predesigned yet man shuns grief.'

A tremor of thrill crosses Mihir's being with this realization of the convergence of human anatomy and philosophy.

'Let me get you some tea. Meanwhile you can read the newspaper. You probably need it for your mains,' Jyoti says as she heads to the kitchen.

Mihir is surprised at her mention of mains and a streak of joy crosses his heart at the thought that she knows. A sense of reciprocity, wrapped in a blend of empathy, attraction, desire and possessiveness fills in him. 'Am I falling into a trap of love? God knows what it is! No matter how insufficient man's description of emotion is, he can never resist the temptation to name it.'

'Don't worry. No formalities, please. If you start with all this I will feel very guilty.' Mihir puts his hand forward to get her to sit down.

'I will also have tea with you; we have to drink and eat something to get going. It's not a big deal so there is no need to feel guilty.' Jyoti heads to the kitchen.

'There is a difference between your tea and my tea. Yours is an everyday thing while mine is a luxury, not a need,' Mihir says philosophically.

Jyoti is in the kitchen. Since Mihir's arrival both their hearts have been beating overtime, pounding with desire. While the amplitude keeps fluctuating in accordance with the interplay of death and desire in the conversation, at no point does the desire get muted.

As he waits, Mihir notices a bookshelf in the room and walks towards it. He sees a few gazettes and contract rule books and then notices some books by Albert Camus. The books afford a peep into her personality. 'I am at Jyoti's who till the other day was so distant. Wait, distant yet close. This is what is bizarre about the whole thing.' He feels butterflies in his stomach but also feels the weight of her father's death. He also feels that wading through the medley of death and desire is a bit of a drain on his mind.

Jyoti joins Mihir and hands him a cup of tea.

'Your father was a government employee?'

'Yes. He retired as a Chief Engineer from CPWD (Central Public Works Department),' Jyoti answers even as the mere mention of her father brings her grief back.

'Does your mother work?' Mihir asks.

'No, she is a housewife. My elder sister teaches at Kendriya Vidyalaya, RK Puram.'

Mihir is tempted to inquire about her sister's marriage but resists.

'That is good. You are writing your JRF. Are you going for your Ph.D?' he asks. Jyoti is happy at Mihir's knowledge and she mentally curses her destiny. 'The first time I am talking to the muse of my desire is because of the death of my father. I think destiny has willed it so that I can learn life by living and enjoy it. Perhaps God is conveying the reality of the eternal incompleteness of life. Mihir has travelled to me on a vehicle of adversity but maybe I am lucky that fate has chosen him whom I desire an anchor in my grief.'

Jyoti is also taking solace in the thought of God to reconcile the contradictions of life and get some hope.

'As of now I do want to pursue my Ph.D, but I don't know how things will work now.'

'Don't worry, it will be okay.'

'This was my father's refuge from work.' Jyoti gestures towards the bookshelf they are standing in front of.

'Albert Camus? So he was inclined towards philosophy?'

'Yes. He loved sharing his reading with us. However, I thought it was too heavy even though by way of History I am not a complete stranger to metaphysics.'

'I have only read some of his work but I know he is impressive and I fully subscribe to his Absurdism. "You will keep finding the meaning of life and the universe but it is not humanly possible to get the final answer." Even my father's favourite theme in Shakespeare's writings is,"Life is full of sound and fury signifying nothing. Life is like a brief candle, a walking shadow." It is in times like this that one can truly appreciate the meaning of these words and ideas. I think these people have done humanity a great service by providing an anchor to man's tumultuous mind.'

'That is true. But then too much of such thoughts start driving me crazy. I get scared and come back into this trail of motion.'

'Right. I think it is only meant to sublimate your intense emotions. Apart from being an art, life is a science as well that has to be negotiated in the right ways.'

Mihir notices that Jyoti has started crying again. She tries to hide it but bursts out, 'Mummy is all alone to battle it out.'

'No way. Both her daughters are bold and strong. You are both pursuing your careers and I am sure you are adept at managing worldly affairs. Yes, the emotional trauma has to be battled but as a History girl, I know you will manage it by dabbling in some philosophy.' Mihir nudges her to console her. He feels an instant stir. At his touch Jyoti falls onto Mihir's chest, her hands resting on his shoulders,and melts into sobs. This is a thawing of frosted emotions, their chemistry finally coming to life. Mihir is frozen, his hands suspended in mid-air for an incomplete embrace. Jyoti can sense his hesitance and she brings her arms around him in an embrace, resting her full body on him. Mihir then completes the embrace, both of them revelling in the resonance of their emotions, desire and possessiveness. Both stand frozen in their embrace, Mihir affectionately caressing Jyoti's hair, those springy tresses which often set his heart aflutter, but which now lie smothered by sadness.

Mihir thinks, 'Desire playing out under the shadow of death; the hue of the room is perfectly Mona Lisa.'

'I won't say that everything is all right but it will be,' Mihir says, his words getting impeded by his overwhelming emotions. This is certainly not the coming together of two strangers. Though their desire is doused by tears and grief, it is throbbing with consistency. They both are listening to each other's pounding hearts. They fall silent. The continuing pause amplifies their desire till the world around gets muted. Passion has soared to command their minds and they turn captives to its diktat.

They both move towards the sofa but then Jyoti guides Mihir to her room. Just as they are about to enter, suddenly the enchantment of passion is lifted and the hug gets broken.

Neither knows who released whom first. They stand apart for a few bewildered moments before Mihir sits down, shying away from Jyoti.

Mihir thinks guiltily, 'I almost fell headlong into desire and made love to a bereaved girl. Till just a while back, I was apprehensive of even responding to Jyoti, lest I should get hijacked off my path to ambition. Uday counselled me to just dabble with desire without sinking into the senti hanky-panky, and here destiny has directly catapulted me into desire surrounded by emotion. Can I walk out without any emotional baggage or can I balance both like Sandeep? This has happened at the critical juncture of my mains. I don't have time to let the turbulence find its natural passage without it eating into my studies. But Jyoti might have been uplifted by this encounter; she looked tired of being sad.'

Jyoti is also guilt-ridden. 'Was I sinning? Doing something like this when I have just lost my father?' But still her face is wearing a sheen of rejuvenation. She further thinks, 'If life has to move on, this is perfectly timed. It's good that we didn't go ahead because I would be tormented by guilt; but even this splash into passion has flushed some grief out of me. It is probably destiny which has delivered to me my desire in the guise of my father's death.'

A brief pause makes both of them feel awkward. Speech comes to their rescue.

'Will you eat something? You must be hungry.' Jyoti breaks the silence and inches towards Mihir.

'No thanks. I think I should leave now.'

'That's not fair. You didn't tell me anything about your family. I think I deserve to know something about you.' Jyoti sits down but they feel an exciting unease every time they look at each other.

They talk for some time and Mihir tells her about himself.

After a while, Mihir assertively seeks her leave and departs. His mind is a medley of thoughts of death and desire. By the time he gets home his mind fixates on death. He feels the melancholy in his mind brewing some verses. He thinks, 'Life is futile; for God taking life from one body and injecting it into another body is a sport; the sport of expressing Himself through different identities.' At night when Uday and Sandeep are asleep, Mihir takes out his diary. The verses are streaming out. He talks to God, 'Oh God! If only this futile frenzy was not merely an ephemeral import sucked out to replenish your frenzy for switching identities!'

~

The Debut Flops

The mains have begun and it is their first paper. The trio reaches UPSC, their centre for the exams. Their togetherness is like soma, sedating the butterflies in their stomachs. The entire area is full of boys and girls, sitting, standing and reclining with some parents sitting patiently, patting and caressing their children. They are like miserable heaps, buried into themselves, as if the world outside doesn't exist.

'It appears as if this is the first question she will find in her paper,' Uday says gesturing towards a girl.

'If she doesn't, all the butterflies will break out of her,' Mihir says, feeling guilty.

'They make me realize the demon CS is,' Sandeep says as he takes in the scene.

'Half an hour left. We can ease ourselves by watching them,' Uday says.

'I don't think I am even prepared to go for my second paper. I couldn't even attempt 50 marks straightaway,' Mihir says.

'30 here as well and 10 in Stats that I didn't know, so I'm

in the same boat,' Sandeep replies.

'They say it's a race against time. Even I missed 30 marks in total. The mantra is just to stay afloat,' Uday reassures them.

But the '50 missed in GS-I' haunts Mihir and doesn't allow him to give the other papers with confidence. 'Please keep calm. You know this first time is just a way for you to get experience, so just finish everything,' his mother says in the evening. He manages to stumble through his mains, not even completing his last Anthro. paper. But he has emerged from the mains focused on his next attempt. At times the completeness of loss helps you gain single-mindedness.

For Sandeep, mains getting over does not mean that the job is finished. There is something important still left—the JRF entrance test, just a few days later. He doesn't want to leave behind the option of lectureship, and one can't become a lecturer without clearing this test. He had persuaded Uday and Mihir to fill the form for the exam as well and is now insisting that they show up for the entrance. They agree, as they don't say no to each other. That is how blissfully captivated by their friendship they are.

With mains and JRF over, Uday and Mihir take a break to go home while Sandeep stays back to make up for his lost classes of Medieval India. They meet after Uday and Mihir return.

'I was so guilty at home, seeing my mother so expectant. I was constantly thinking what would happen if everything went wrong,' Uday says seriously.

'I was okay. Mummy has counselled my father also about my just doing this for experience, but Papa, I know, is still watching me keenly,' Mihir says.

'Had I gone home they would have said, "It's only the mains

and ultimately the finals matter; if they too knew how it feels to grab happiness in bits!' Sandeep says. Uday is confident about his mains and his CS cousins have okayed it. Sandeep says he is not sure either way. Mihir is fine with the idea that this attempt is to get a feel of the whole thing. Mihir and Uday attend a few classes and the trio resume their group study for the next prelims. Sandeep and Mihir are focusing on their Anthro., so as usual preparations for CS and MA are going hand in hand. However, this time, with the familiar Medieval History being their option for specialization, there's no chance of a West Asia episode happening to them.

Anthro. and Mihir continue to be strange bedfellows. Mihir is still haunted by different ghosts, Australopithecus, Ramapithecus, etc. He keeps thinking of running away from Anthro. every now and then, but Uday's mantra, 'Some pills are bitter yet have to be swallowed' keeps him stuck to it. While learning the statistics of skeletons, Mihir often thinks, 'If all our ancestors were cremated, these ghosts would not be rising up to haunt me. Is it not enough to learn that our forefathers were apes? How does it benefit us to know their shapes and size to be able to run the Government of India?' Mihir's usual library sojourns have also been revived. The one difference is that the chemistry with Jyoti has been transformed. Their encounter in Jyoti's house was left hanging in the hiatus caused first by Jyoti's absence and then Mihir's, as he was busy with his mains. They have progressed from silence to hellos but the ice is still not fully broken, a strange hesitation present whenever they see each other. With Jyoti it is because of the guilt that her desires welled up immediately after her father's death and for Mihir it is guilt plus shyness. Now there is no ego because the idea of nearly making love to a girl who just lost her father has brought a bizarre mix of empathy and desire. During their conversation that day, Mihir had told Jyoti how he had resolved to hand over all his life's important decisions to his parents. Now he doesn't know if that is also preventing Jyoti from coming back to him since she is intelligent enough to understand that after career, marriage is the only other important subject.

The Sandeep–Aparna pair is peacefully treading the middle path while the Uday–Sanjana duo is still charged with electric sensuality. Uday holds the reins in their relationship. He feels smug about the fact that Sanjana is still his despite his having revealed to her his firm resolve to marry a girl his mother chooses for him. The chemistry of marriage and the chemistry of desire don't always converge probably because desire involves only a duo while marriage involves many.

The anticipation of Holi is building up but this time the impending mains results is playing out like a background music to rein in the excitement.

For Sandeep, this music is louder and more dampening. He is anxious about the impending JRF results. After all, when birds of such different feathers flock together, life is bound to pulsate with varied beats. This time it is Sandeep's turn to beat the drum.

'Tomorrow I will have to go to the university. The JRF and NET results are out,' Sandeep says, feeling like a traitor to CS.

'A dog's tail can never be straight,' Uday sneers at Sandeep.

Mihir as usual plays a balancing act between CS and MA and says, 'We don't need to go with him. Let him go if he wants to.'

'Aren't you curious to see how your inventions have fared

this time? Uday has also devoted two full days to E.H. Carr,' Sandeep says mischievously.

'I never thought knowing "what is history" is far more difficult than knowing history. It was a horrendous reading. By the time you get some sort of grip on what you have read everything goes reeling out. It's like a game of snakes and ladders where just before reaching the end you jump on top of a snake and slither to the bottom,' Uday speaks with a sense of vengeance against E.H. Carr.

Hearing Uday Mihir thinks, 'Like history, knowing "what is life" is far more difficult than living life.'

'It was the bloody philosophy of History and getting stuck on single sentences. Sort of like moving from one square to another after countless throws of the dice.' Mihir takes Uday's metaphor forward. 'That is why I went from one heading to another, leaving the task of bridging up the gaps to my imagination; there are a few things in life which fall in place only when you throw them to the winds.'

Sandeep says to Uday sarcastically, 'That means there is full scope for him getting through with great marks again.'

Mihir is amused, reminded of what he wrote in the exam. 'History is not the chronicling of facts, it is the interpretation of facts. Carr says that the selection of facts and their interpretation depend upon the type and personality of the historian. In simple terms, neither facts nor interpretation is absolute and the variety of humans on earth makes history a matter of innumerable permutations and combinations. Our inheritance decides our belief. Massive research is the need of the hour, if we dare.'

The next day the trio go to the university, despite Uday's

unwillingness. It's exactly like the last time with Sandeep at the notice board and Mihir and Uday slightly behind him.

'He is a real monster who plucks fruits out of nowhere,' Sandeep says.

'Is it the West Asia episode repeated?' Uday asks, looking at Mihir, feigning anger but smiling at the same time.

'Yes. He is on the NET list,' Sandeep says, mimicking Uday's half-angry half-fun tone.

'What about Sandy? He won't tell us about his result,' Mihir says, going towards the notice board.

'No need to check. I am in the JRF list,' Sandeep says guiltily.

Uday says, 'I had not even completed the paper. This is a bonanza. Both of you need to give treats.'

'Treat? Me? Mine is a mere NET without any fellowship. But Sandy with a 55 in the exams and now JRF deserves to give a lavish one,' Mihir smiles at Sandeep. Mihir is reminded of how during his last visit to Delhi his father had said, 'It is frightening to see people settle for JRF under the dazzle of suddenly found financial freedom. Don't get into that trap. It could make you complacent.'

Before the JRF beat begins fading, the crescendo of mains begins echoing; the results could come in any day.

The group is at Batra and the motorcycles raise the same razzmatazz and anticipation in those left behind, since the mains results are out. This time the trio's caravan fetches only one name, Uday's. He grows visibly ecstatic but controls his emotions because of his friends' failure; it's like a brilliant sun getting obscured by the wintry haze. Uday remains quiet and so do Sandeep and Mihir. Only silence can soothe the unease. The situation demands they feel happy for Uday. Mihir thinks,

'Ah, this situation is a perfect Mona Lisa one! Feeling sad can also be so difficult!' Sandeep's JRF compensates his deficit, a Buddhist balancing on the middle path. Mihir's cultivated calmness is tinged with envy. Mihir thinks, 'He dictates desire and is now balancing CS, dharma and desire with equal elan. And me? I am envying my friend. I am sensitive in my head but not when it's actually required. Then again, being envious is normal, what is pathological is its malefic manifestation. Uday's mother deserves his success.' Mihir feels complacent in thinking of Uday's mother. He continues thinking about CS, 'Efforts or no efforts, at the time of results one grows expectant. "Ah! what if!" That's because they say in the CS world miracles abound; but miracles are more heard than seen. I will scale up my karma for CS.'

As it happens, man tends to settle into the changed hue of life, happy or sad. Uday is appearing for his interview, Sandeep is organizing himself better to plug the loopholes of his first attempt without losing sight of his MA, since a 55 with JRF holds him in good stead for a DU lectureship, and Mihir is bracing himself to go the whole hog for his next attempt. In this changed scenario, sadness from failure and a sense of resolve find a cosy coexistence in Mihir's mind.

It's Holi again but the colours of Holi are different for Uday, Sandep and Mihir. The bonhomie of togetherness has brewed a CS soma which has rendered its magic, transporting everyone into a trance. The colour of their Holi becomes one again. Finally, it becomes a Jumma Chumma Holi again

'The final results are out! What of Uday?' Ajit comes home screaming while Mihir is lying in bed struggling with the statistics of his ancestors' skeletons. Sandeep has gone back to his home in Ranchi after his MA finals. Uday has planned to receive his final results at Patna with his mother.

'When?' Mihir asks.

'Just a while back. Alok told me,' Ajit says.

'Let me check with Aslam since he also appeared in the interview. Uday gave him his roll number knowing it would be the fastest way.' Mihir gets ready to leave.

Mihir and Ajit hurry to Aslam's house in front of Batra. The commotion on the road says everything. Opposite his flat at the pan shop, they see Aslam talking to a few boys and his face conveys his fate of not making it. Aslam shakes his head signalling a no since he knows Uday lives with Mihir.

'Not in the list. So far there are only two from MN on the list,' Aslam says, visibly distressed.

'Does Uday know?' Mihir asks.

'I haven't told him yet.'

'I think we should tell him,' Ajit proposes.

Mihir phones Uday and without wasting any time, tells him the news. Uday remains silent.

'This is only your first time and getting through to the interview in the first attempt is not a joke,' Mihir tells Uday. The line disconnects, the click conveying Uday's heart.

'They are right when they say it's a dangerous and slippery road.' Ajit sounds sad.

'I wonder how he is feeling. Positive after a good interview, he left for Patna to share his excitement with his mother.' Mihir knows that one's success is reflected in the faces of one's parents and he thinks of his father who has been his passionate companion in shutting all the other doors for him to concentrate on CS.

The scene changes again with the trio appearing for the prelims the second time. This life doesn't afford the luxury of mourning.

~

The Trio Disperses

The soma of togetherness catapults the trio to take life head on. They make it through the prelims with no issues and are set on their mains. With the MA under their belt, there is no speed breaker to retard their CS pace. In the changed circumstances, Sandeep, with the JRF in his pocket, has ensured his continued stay in Delhi, independent of his father and brother. But for Mihir the NET holds no value; his world begins and ends with CS. 'Interview right in the first attempt', has now turned into a positive motivation for Uday, bringing the CS within attainable limits. He is like a wounded tiger on the prowl. Aparna, Sanjana and Jyoti are now teeming rather than blazing in the trio's lives.

'I think Anthro. was a big blunder. It still sends me into a trance and I can't help cursing all those buriers. These chimpanzees are howling at my CS prospects, I can't cram the stats of their skulls, it is just doing an "Ajit" on me,' Mihir complains to Uday and Sandeep. Failures lend you insight into your weaknesses.

'For God's sake, stop being emotional about what you read! Be a professional and focus on why you are reading it. Changing optional would mean losing the advantage of what is already done,' Uday counsels with his trademark clarity.

'And you are not Ajit. For him everything is Anthro.,' Sandeep says, smiling.

'But if science is so sure about chimpanzees being our forefathers, why does the idea of Adam and Eve still persist?' Mihir wonders aloud.

'To keep God alive,' Uday sneers.

'I think Mihir should have opted for philosophy. That affords ample scope for shooting intel fundas—you are free to make God existent and non-existent at the same time,' Sandeep says.

'But only factual questions get high scores. It is not wise to bring fiction into CS. The strategy is to play safe to score high,' Uday says with elan.

'You mean to say the study of God is fiction?' Sandeep questions.

'Here I agree with Uday. God may be a risky venture in CS. Suppose I resort to my imagination for an unprepared question and I shoot God but the evaluator turns out to be a theist or vice-versa, he may end up shooting me as a CS aspirant. When it comes to God, many can't detach themselves and judge things objectively,' Mihir says.

'Yes, so keep your tryst with God limited to deriving the hope soma from Him to fight the demons of life,' Uday says.

'You sound like a hardcore utilitarian who doesn't even spare God,' Sandeep says.

'Even God is a utilitarian who uses man to enjoy His existence without having to be visible on earth, if at all He is even there,' Uday says.

'I agree. It has always been like that. In Anthro., religion says man saw God in everything he found useful,' Sandeep says.

'Here I am struggling with horrific chimpanzees and you two are enjoying the luxury of a discourse on God. Let Him remain in heaven and you come down to earth, He can't stop these chimpanzees from scaring me. But I can't help feeling surprised at the disparity in CS with high-scoring subjects being at par with the risky ones. They say simply learning grammar and facts by heart made many clear CS.' Mihir seems in awe of his forefathers.

Absolutely correct. They should have one standard yardstick for all. GS should be the only paper, thus making the science students study humanities and vice-versa, in order to churn out true generalists,' Sandeep supports Mihir.

'I just don't believe in wasting time in what is beyond me,' Uday has the last word.

The trio are approaching their second mains attempt, leaving the first one far behind. But it suddenly comes to the fore again as they receive their marksheets for their first attempt.

'Shit man! What have I done to myself?' Mihir falls on the bed, having opened his marksheet.

'What happened?' Sandeep asks.

'167 in GS-I! I had missed 50 marks in that. And the total is just short of the mains cutoff. 240 even in Anthro. which I deliberately massacred. 128 in essay is a bit reassuring since my flair for writing got me through. Just holding my nerve would have gotten me through,' Mihir is depressed and remorseful.

'Mine is a bigger surprise. 278 in History and 340 in Pub. Ad. GS-I is only 135, though I missed only 30. The interview was okay with 165. My knowledge of CS is topsy-turvy. I was working harder on Pub. Ad. I missed quite bit in that.' Uday is worried.

'In my case everything is predictable except the 180 in Anthro-I. The overall is well short of the cutoff. I knew I hadn't done well in GS, especially the second paper.' Sandeep says calmly.

'It's like practising with a javelin for the discus throw.' Uday is annoyed.

Seeing Uday depressed makes Mihir dizzy. He feels completely deflated in utter repentance, thinking, 'Alas! If I had just written my papers properly.'

'You should feel encouraged by getting so close. This is why experienced guys preach to stay afloat,' Sandeep counsels Mihir.

'But this was my last chance free from the shadow of reservations. The next one could mean the improvement getting neutralized by the lesser seats available.' Mihir is inconsolable.

'Stop worrying about what is to come.' Uday has taken control again. 'The mantra is to stay afloat. CS also seems to be proving Lord Krishna right. Just work without bothering about the fruits.'

'You are detached? No way! You said "I will conquer CS; it is ours". What is all this?' Sandeep retorts.

'Yes, I am. If at all one has to stay afloat we need to gather all the buoyancy possible. What is the point of hitting turbulent waters with leaking sails?' Uday is back to his old self.

The reason in Uday's arguments appeals to Mihir. He gets up and says to Uday, 'I don't know if these words were actually uttered by Krishna to Arjuna or are merely ascribed to him but here you are the one saying them to me, so for me you are being a Krishna.'

'So sentimental. But really well said,' Sandeep says to Mihir, looking fondly at him.

Mihir wonders, 'When did I become so expressive? The deluge of emotions unleashed by life can demolish even the most stubborn shyness.'

Life is again settling into a changed hue. CS is making these boys adept at negotiating the rapidly shifting hues in life.

Sandeep has enrolled for an M.Phil while Mihir and Uday focus only on CS.

The mains examination has begun and the boys have entered confidently with only Mihir still unsure about Anthro. They have done reasonably well in their papers. Overall they have done better and what did not go well is taken with a philosophical 'It's normal in CS.' Mihir is nervous about not describing his forefathers accurately and about his bad handwriting. Uday says he has delivered his best and it is now destiny's turn to deliver. Sandeep is an inherent optimist who thinks his positives will outweigh his negatives.

Uday goes home after the exams since he is always conscious of his mother being alone at home and Mihir also goes home. Mihir's father has retired from the service so he is now guilty about his being at Delhi. The same old snapshot grows larger in his mind; his father giving tuitions to manage his stay in Delhi, his elder sister not getting married because of inadequate dowry and the delay making dowry amounts higher; his mother growing discontented because her small world howls at her and the 'like father like son' pressure keeps mounting. Mihir thinks about his sister's marriage, 'This is the sort of inflation for which man can't blame the government. In Anthro. I am studying how societies came into being to meet man's needs and here this social institution of dowry is coming in the way of the fulfilment of man's needs. I want to be in the civil services because society respects it and I want my parents to bask in that social glory. Society is powerful. It sculpts our dreams and determines our aspirations.'

Sandeep has also taken a break to go to Ranchi. With his stay in Delhi now independent of his parents and brother because of his fellowship, he is now closer to his love and is even contemplating rebellion for Aparna in case CS betrays him. Money gives you the courage to rebel against the tradition.

They have timed their reunion after Holi and before the mains results.

The results have been declared, the noise at Batra this time exploding with a whimper since none of the three have made it through mains. They are dumbstruck. They reach their flat on autopilot mode; habits help you when you are out of your mind. Uday and Mihir go to bed, buried in their thoughts. Sandeep is in the verandah. They have not exchanged even a word with each other. Silence can speak and convey the absoluteness of the adversity. The night has been bad with them being frightened of the monster in front of them and sleep evading them. Even when they manage to doze off, hardly a few minutes pass before they spring back into consciousness. That is how they negotiate the night. When morning comes they feel like the world should end and end their misery.

Uday makes an announcement, 'I am shifting back to Patna. I have told my folks at home.'

'No third chance?' Mihir asks.

'I will consider that later. Right now I can't tax my mother anymore. So far MA was my compelling reason to be in Delhi.

I have given my best to CS, and what is lacking will always remain lacking,' Uday says with the painful knowledge that the trio will be split.

'Even I will have to shift back to the hostel. Being with the JRF people will be the only way I can learn where to get guides who can get me a lectureship. It is something I badly want because going back to Ranchi means leaving Aparna behind. CS is a risky venture but I will continue with it. I have anyway been a Buddhist in my desire for CS; okay if I get it, otherwise I'll go for JRF,' Sandeep tells Mihir guiltily.

'Even I can't spoil my peace for this CS. I can have a go at it with care-a-damn attitude, but I have to consider my other options. I have to support my mother and now if I am not keen on DU for lectureship, Patna is as good as Delhi. But yes, I will miss us as a group,' Uday the lion is damning the den for refusing to allow him in twice.

Mihir thinks of the dissolution of the trio, 'Compulsions of life tend to consume the fun.'

'Mihir, what about you?' Sandeep asks.

'I think getting away is beyond me. It's either this or nothing else, and that means waiting till I exhaust all of my chances. Even if I do want to quit, my father will not let me. He will advise me to remain saddled to my ambition no matter how bumpy the ride. So let me see how it works out,' Mihir says, feeling pained at their world being destroyed.

'But without Sandeep and me around?' Uday is concerned.

'I will look for single accommodation. Being with somebody else after having you guys will be…' Mihir tries hiding his pain.

'But we have to remain in touch with each other,' Sandeep says, looking at Uday.

'I will be around. You know me. And the road to Sitagarh passes through Patna,' Uday says to Mihir, but his booming voice is now mellow.

'But we are here this month. Maybe even a little longer because of hostel formalities,' Sandeep looks at Uday for his consent.

'Sure! That means twenty more days.' Uday pats Mihir's back to cheer him up.

'It seems like just the other day when we were hunting for a place to stay and making it a home. Today we are parting unfulfilled.' Mihir is sinking into melancholia. He thinks, 'It is a moment of total loss. No CS, no more friends, no more soma, no more high. Life seems so grim. Alas! If life could again do a Mona Lisa to me, infusing some radiance into this total darkness. Even if the order is perfect, brewing an absolute happiness, one is scared if something goes wrong. Any change in such a state can only make one sadder. The impending loneliness is illuminating the worth of togetherness. Things become precious only when they aren't there anymore.'

As of now, CS has taken a backseat. It's a few days before Uday's scheduled departure.

'Sanjana has stormed her way into my heart now when I am leaving her,' Uday is talking to himself.

'Ha ha ha. It's easier said than done. Living in togetherness without an emotional trail is like being an asura, which you are not. You are a proclaimed Krishna. He abducted Rukmini to make her his wife. So where is this Krishna?' Sandeep has a go at Uday.

'But he also left Radha for his higher responsibilities and I have already said that Sanjana is Radha,' Uday counters.

'You say she has stormed into your heart. You can make Radha Rukmini. Why don't you ask your mother for approval? Maybe…' Mihir intervenes.

'No way. I know her views on marriage. Also I couldn't clear CS for her, so I can't ask her for anything. Dharma and desire don't meet that easily,' Uday explains.

'But why mix love and ambition, dharma and desire? Here you sound like a communist, like Mihir, sacrificing your love for your mother and maybe CS too. Then again at least you dabbled in desire. Mihir doesn't even enter desire, so love stands ruled out,' Sandeep says.

Mihir is reminded of his desire-filled encounter with Jyoti in her flat and a sense of guilt pierces his heart. 'I haven't told my best friends about what happened but they know I am incorrigibly shy.'

'Here I am a bit like your Ganesha. My mother is my world. But Ganesha had both of his parents…' Uday says sombrely. 'To my relief they have made Gods support all kinds of logic otherwise Sandy would constantly knock me down.'

'That is still there so accept you are not an ardent follower of Krishna.' Sandeep is persistent.

'I am still Krishna. I have already clarified that Krishna will always get you something. He is truly exciting and was privileged to have both Rukmini and Radha. Krishna gives justification for all human deeds because he was human and he was a Leo.' Uday revels again in his zodiac association. 'Sandeep, here you are abductor Krishna, rebelling against all for Anjana, even though her parents don't agree.'

Mihir thinks, 'Uday is right. Krishna is there for all human deeds. Even he has turned into a Krishna, and they don't know about my having turned into a Krishna as well. They say Krishna had a secret union with Radha, like I with Jyoti, though momentary; what else was that passionate hug at Jyoti's?'

'Like you had displayed the human deed of Pandava revenge against Brijesh—spray of desire returned with the torrential rain of passions,' Sandeep says mischievously.

Mihir says philosophically, 'Man tends to invoke a justification for his actions and God affords an irrefutable justification. But actually all of us are unique amalgams and no one is exactly like someone else.'

'Yes, you are definitely unique. In this world of Krishna, you are a perfect Shiva to Jyoti, making her wait endlessly,' Uday says and the flat reverberates with the boisterous laughter of the trio after a long time. However, 'Shiva' stirs Mihir again.

~

Jyoti Rises Again

The trio are at the station platform and they hear the train's final whistles. Uday rushes to get into the train and keeps looking back at Sandeep and Mihir, smiling despite the pangs of departure. The last whistle pushes the train away and creates a void in Mihir and Sandeep.

'Now it's your turn,' Mihir sighs.

'I am here in Delhi itself,' Sandeep tries to reassure him.

Mihir thinks, 'When the world changes, distances become unbridgeable.'

'But...that is not the same,' Mihir replies.

Mihir and Sandeep get to their flat. CS has taken a back seat. They have decided to go for a movie at Batra to deal with their sadness after Uday's departure. They don't sleep too well and the next day Sandeep goes to explore options for a hostel room while Mihir begins his search for single accommodation.

Mihir's father is visiting Delhi; after two failed attempts, knowing his son is depressed, he wants to give his son some comfort. Sandeep has managed to find a hostel room for himself and will be moving in the next month, leaving Mihir alone in the flat till he finds an alternative accommodation. His father tells him, 'Do not worry about paying the rent for a month or so.'

'I have already spoken to Sudhir and some more people I know to help with the search for accommodation for you,' Sandeep tells Mihir before he leaves. 'And rest assured we will meet frequently. You know I am a Buddhist who knows how to strike a balance.'

Hearing Sandeep talk about Buddhism, Mihir is reminded of Uday's Krishna.

'Yes that goes without saying but what about your next CS attempt?' Mihir feels weird about the quick changes.

'We are all giving the prelims anyway so the next attempt is the fait accompli,' Sandeep says. 'Actually let me tell you about the pressures on me. Aparna has completed her B.Ed. and is likely to get a teaching assignment soon. Her parents have started talking about marriage. I still don't have my family's approval. I thought I would be able to win them over if I get into the civil services but now that is also uncertain. So I need this JRF fellowship so that I can marry her.'

'I heard you are vacating the flat. Alok just told me because I only got back today,' Ajit says as he enters.

'Come in, Ajit. It's good to see you after so long. Looks like Alok is enjoying his success,' Sandeep says.

'What success? He is likely to get the Central Secretariat Services in his third attempt. He was expecting more but is at peace,' Ajit says as he sits down.

'Is he writing the exam again?' Mihir asks.

'Yes but he will join the services and write alongside. He says he feels guilty about taxing his parents.'

'What about you?' Sandeep asks Ajit.

'Enough of CS. When even the generals are getting slain in the battlefield what can one say about a sepoy like me? After Alok leaves, I will shift to Ashok Vihar with one of my college mates who is also pursuing the Company Secretary course,' Ajit says calmly. 'You people are shifting? Where is Uday?'

They tell him the story.

'Just a few days back, both our flats resonated with bonhomie and now...life changes so fast!' Ajit is pensive, this time not about answering a prelims question but answering the puzzle of life. 'Mihir! I know of a single accommodation, a sort of barsati that's available. It's not very costly as it's just a single room. One of my friends, Suresh, was mentioning it to me just the other day. You will have some company too since Suresh lives on the first floor. He is pursuing CS wholeheartedly since for him it is either CS or business. He comes from a rich business family so CS for him is a passion not tainted by a sense of survival.' Mihir is relieved at the prospect of escaping the property dealers. He then thinks, 'Property dealers are absolutely following a middle path, striking a profit balance between landlords and tenants.' He is reminded of Sandeep's 'middle path' and a streak of nostalgia with a dash of humour crosses his mind and tickles his sombre self into a faint smile for a fleeting moment.

Mihir is not in a hurry to go to sleep. At times shutting your eyes brings the whole world in, and if you keep them open the world is served to the mind in slices. For him the present world is too frightening to be called in as a whole at once. He is thinking, 'The trio was an orchestra and now, even with Sandeep still here, the two of us can't recreate even a bit of that symphony; the chemistry of life doesn't follow the theory that the whole is the sum of the parts.' Mihir's mind jumps to the arrival of his father...and then his next CS attempt...and then on to the path of dreary diligence without any hope of indulging in the soma of bonhomie. Jyoti suddenly crosses his gloomy mind, leaving a trail of pleasure amidst pain. The hue changes from dark to Mona Lisa.

With Sandeep gone the next day, Mihir is alone in the flat waiting for Ajit. They have planned to go to Suresh's place to figure out Mihir's accommodation. Ajit arrives, they set out, meet Suresh, meet the landlord and everything is settled successfully. Mihir will shift on the 15th of the month.

Mihir and Ajit fall into nostalgia, chatting about CS and walking to Batra. They are trying to lose themselves in the hustle and bustle of the outer world.

Mihir's father arrives. Though he tries to hide it, his concern for his son is visible. To Mihir this is apparent since he is the cause of concern; the empathy is not only about realizing what the other one feels but also what the other one doesn't show. Mihir and his father are not talking much, their silence communicating their story.

'You said you are not feeling comfortable with Anthro. Why don't you change your optional this time?' Mihir's father asks.

'They say managing a new optional without dropping the chance is a risky venture,' Mihir replies.

'But you said a major part of Anthro. is common to Sociology. One of my very intimate friends just retired from JNU as a Sociology professor. We talk to each other often; we studied together in Allahabad University. If you want, let me know, I can take you to him for some guidance.' Mihir's father gauges his reaction.

Mihir pauses for a moment and thinks about the offer. He is attracted to the idea of a one-on-one interaction.

'Okay. There is no harm in meeting him and knowing his views,' Mihir says.

'Then let's go this evening itself. You have arranged your accommodation so don't worry about the rental money going up a bit,' his father is still trying to assuage Mihir's fears.

They go to Prof. Sharma's house in the evening.

'What a pleasant surprise!' Prof. Sharma and Mihir's father hug.

They talk about various subjects and then finally they get to the point of the visit. Mihir's father explains the context.

'In fact, after retiring, I am looking forward to providing professional guidance to a few students for the civil services. Even in JNU they are mad about CS. This will keep affording me the company of students and that way my void will be managed better,' Prof. Sharma says.

'So do you advise him to switch to Sociology?'

'Of course. If he is not comfortable with Anthro., he should switch. I am here to help and a considerable part of Anthro. overlaps with Sociology, which is an advantage. He can get started right away with me,' Prof. Sharma assures them.

'Mihir, what do you think?' Mihir's father asks.

''Yes, with Sir here to guide me, I am ready.' Mihir is excited at the prospect of getting rid of Anthro.

Prof. Sharma then asks Mihir about his studies and scores so far.

'Don't mind but I'll talk a bit about Sociology to you. It's how I start working with a student,' Prof. Sharma says.

'Absolutely. For us teachers the student's impression decides the attitude,' Mihir's father agrees.

'Son, since you have already studied quite a bit of Socio in Anthro, can you tell me what you think Sociology is?' Prof. Sharma asks Mihir.

After a moment's pause, Mihir answers, 'Sociology is the study of the development, structure and functioning of human society and human social behaviour. Most importantly it covers the dynamics of the interaction between the individual and his society.'

'What do you mean by the dynamics of individual–society interaction?' Prof. Sharma probes.

'It basically implies the study of how social institutions are able to manage an individual's human emotions and to what extent balance has been struck between individual freedom and social order,' Mihir explains.

'Can you elaborate this individual–society matrix a bit more?' Prof. Sharma goes deeper.

'Sir, it is like the feelings of a boy in school, a member in a family... Sociologists study the various models of social institutions including the family, where man doesn't get dehumanized under the stifling social order,' Mihir answers.

'Do you think political ideology also has a bearing on social order?' Prof. Sharma is in teacher mode.

'Yes Sir, no political ideology or order is independent of social implications. It is basically always a socio-political order, in fact a socio-economic-political order. For example in the communist USSR which has recently crumbled, the skeletons of individual repression are tumbling out of the cupboards; a society where the citizens had no voice, no human rights and no individual freedom. I mean to say that how a person feels in his society considerably depends upon the way the state is governed,' Mihir is completely absorbed in the subject while his father is an attentive audience, a bit smug that his son is able to hold the attention of Prof. Sharma well.

Prof. Sharma snaps the train of conversation.

'This boy is fit to get into the civil services. His comprehension is very clear and what I liked the most was his definition of sociology. In the bookish definition the dimension of the balance between individual and society is not brought out explicitly.'

Prof. Sharma's words encourage Mihir, raising his self-esteem, which had taken a nosedive after his failed CS attempts. Prof. Sharma assures Mihir's father that he will start his guidance right away and also offers Mihir the unoccupied room on the top floor of his house. But due to the hassle of shifting and the obvious comfort of staying amidst the CS crowd, Mihir decides against it. Mihir's father advises him to spend a few days with Prof. Sharma in order to catch up on the Sociology he has missed and also to honour his offer. Prof. Sharma and Mihir's father then start walking down memory lane and recall how Allahabad University was once acclaimed as a CS-minting university. Their friendship reminds Mihir of his trio. After dinner at Prof. Sharma's, Mihir decides to return to his house after a week to stay for a few days.

Thus Mihir's father gives him the much-needed push on the path to his cherished destination. Mihir's apprehension temporarily subsides. He has shifted to his new accommodation and even struck a friendly equation with Suresh, who remains his only refuge out of his loneliness, as Sudhir has also shifted to the hostel. Mihir's inherent reserved demeanour is an eternal obstacle for him in making friends easily, so Suresh cannot completely fill the void. Though Mihir guards his privacy and loves his solitude, he feels lonely; there is a thin line between solitude and loneliness; solitude is exhilarating, loneliness exilic.

For the first few days Mihir is constantly thinking of his friends and he misses them terribly. He is left desperately hungry for a vibrant chemistry. Jyoti has anyway been constantly buzzing inside him with a fluctuating amplitude and now his loneliness amplifies his need for her. Her luscious form keeps coming to his mind. Mona Lisa springs up again. 'I shunned such a beautiful chemistry, gripped under the spell of my complex. I have been ruthless,' Mihir's mind is back in Jyoti's drawing room where their passionate hug still makes him pulsate with passion. Desire for Jyoti is rising in Mihir at this juncture when he is delicately positioned in his CS; at times only after the trigger is pulled do you realize the fire in the bullet.

Mihir is left hankering for Jyoti and his mind has soared beyond questioning why. The library used to be their haunt but Jyoti's completing her MA and Mihir's baptism into CS preparation terminated their meetings. Mihir is frantic about how to meet her, constantly haunted by the heart-wrenching thought, 'If only I could take the hug forward!' His heart is furiously rising to engulf a resolved mind. 'Is Jyoti still keen on me? What if she is hurt by my indifference? What are her expectations? I have explained my inability to get married to her but will she be able to appreciate that?' His mind is still full of questions and doubts. But the heart wants what it wants and his longing for Jyoti becomes desperate. He wants to see her once or even know of her. He doesn't even know her number. That is when he decides to go to Football, thinking only he can help in the matter of girls; discovery springs from necessity. Jyoti's JRF gives him the hope that he may be able to hunt her out in the DU campus. He wants to meet her before he goes to Prof. Sharma. The thought of 'Prof. Sharma' and 'Sociology' creeps in to breed some guilt, but it does not stay long. He is all set to meet Jyoti.

'Hello, Mihir! You have just disappeared,' Navin aka Football welcomes Mihir.

'I haven't disappeared. I'm right here,' Mihir replies, knowing that he will have to bear with Football to get his help.

'Yes you CS people are big people! How come you remembered me today? You coming here means only one thing.'

'Okay okay, stop teasing. How are you?'

'I am okay. Pursuing UP PCS.'

'What about the others in the batch?' Mihir guides the conversation towards Jyoti.

'Rashmi has gone back, you know…' Football says. Mihir thinks, 'I knew he would begin talking about other girls.' Mihir is reminded of Uday saying that whenever he met Football, 'Somehow when he proclaims himself to be a Kishan Kanhaiya, I feel like abandoning my Krishna.'

After he names three or four girls, Mihir is impatient. Finally Football gets to Jyoti and reveals, 'She often comes to Prof. Shalini Mukherjee, whom she wants as her guide. She comes to the campus for her M.Phil and never fails to ask about you, but knowing you I didn't tell her anything.' Mihir has decided to devote his pre-Prof. Sharma week to Jyoti but the incorrigible cerebral creature that he is, he thinks, 'Am I following Jyoti? Now I can understand what it feels like to be in the throes of desperation for someone. Is she still keen on me? Experience teaches true empathy. Alas! If I had allowed my tryst with her in the drawing room to bloom.' His desire for Jyoti gets further propped up. At this moment desire is completely dominating dharma.

The following day Mihir sets out for the campus, wondering how to explain his presence there. He heads to the library to lend some semblance of purpose to his visit. He is disappointed that in spite of his covering all her probable haunts, Jyoti is not to be seen. Gripped by restlessness he goes and meets Sandeep.

The next day Mihir goes to the university again and he sees Jyoti coming out of the library as he is entering it. The butterfly-like response of Mihir to the sight of Jyoti is unchanged despite that fateful passionate hug. But now Mihir is focused on overcoming his shyness and instead of running away when he sees Jyoti he stays and smiles at her.

'Hi!' Mihir stops Jyoti.

'Hi! How are you?' Jyoti's smile is sparkling on her pink lips; her full-sleeved top flared casually over her wraparound makes Mihir's head spin. He turns smug thinking, 'Ah! such a beautiful girl has been showering me with her attention.'

'Fine. Entangled in CS.' Mihir tries to stay calm.

'It's good that I didn't get into that trap. I always knew it would be scary but I know you are a capable guy.' Jyoti continues smiling but Mihir feels a little sad that Jyoti knows his struggles with CS.

'Let's not talk about CS. What about you? On with your Ph.D?' Mihir asks, looking into Jyoti's eyes.

'Yes. The Ph.D is giving me the blues. First the guide and then the painstaking thesis...'

'Guides know how to ease the Ph.D process. I guess you

know the tricks of the trade by now and girls anyway are cool customers at managing people and the world,' Mihir smiles sarcastically with mischief in his eyes. It seems like their chemistry has calmed down because of the mundane conversation.

'What do you mean?' Jyoti chides Mihir.

'Anyway, what brings you here?'

'Actually I came to meet Sandeep but he was not there. I've been feeling quite lonely after both of them left,' Mihir feels a little guilty at the lie, thinking that Jyoti might actually have liked to know that he was looking for her.

Mihir asks Jyoti to join him for coffee in the canteen. Jyoti blushes and Mihir is also a little embarrassed as they both remember how she used to time her coffee with Mihir's in the past. Jyoti tells Mihir that she is heading to MN to meet an M.Phil friend. Mihir asks her out to lunch at Zen. Jyoti is pleasantly surprised at Mihir's interest in her and her heart is instantly set aflutter. They are both still infatuated with each other; some chemistries are too sparkling to subside.

'In that case I will finish up faster.'

'Let's say we meet at Batra at 1.30?'

'Sure. But I hope you won't mind if I am a few minutes late.'

'Not at all!' Mihir says.

They get to Batra and Mihir sees Jyoti off to her friend's place. Finally they are at Zen. They order veg manchurian and fried rice with Mirinda; Mihir has sacrificed non-vegetarian food knowing Jyoti is a vegetarian. They feel uneasy again but start talking.

'So how is everything at home? I mean your mother and your sister.'

'My Mom is okay now. She's getting used to being without Papa. Didi is also fine and she'll be getting married soon. She had delayed it because...' Jyoti turns sombre. 'Are you looking to do something else too?'

Mihir tells her everything including his single-mindedness about CS, instantly bringing her closer. He also tells her how his father is morally supporting him in his venture.

'And how is your philosophy and fiction reading going on? That day I got to know your love for reading,' Jyoti says as they eat.

'CS hardly gives me any time. More importantly my mind is sort of enslaved to this addiction. I only manage to read occasionally. I hope to enjoy it when life permits. In the recent past I have read only two books.' Mihir laments his lack of time like a hungry hound who can't eat despite food being placed in front of him.

'If you don't mind, may I see your collection? I'm curious even though I am not a keen reader.'

'Sure, by all means.' Mihir feels tossed into happiness at Jyoti's interest.

'How far away is your place?'

'Pretty close by.' Mihir is apprehensive of Suresh seeing him with Jyoti.

They finish eating and Mihir pays the bill. As they approach the flat, Mihir feels butterflies in his stomach, the memory of the hug in Jyoti's apartment instantly travelling to his mind. They reach his room and he is relieved that Suresh isn't around. Mihir offers Jyoti the only chair in the room, gives her a glass of water and sits on his bed.

'You have set up your room pretty well. It's quite unlike

a bachelor's with the lampshade and the wallpaper…' Jyoti is visibly impressed. She appears calm and composed. Mihir thinks, 'My complex is truly pathological; I am so nervous while a girl appears completely at ease sitting alone with me.'

'Yeah. I like my surroundings to be neat and I love the soothing hue created by the lampshade,' Mihir explains.

'Now, can I see your collection?'

'Yes, sure,' Mihir takes Jyoti to his bookshelf, an open cupboard with many shelves.

'Wow, so many books!' Jyoti looks at the books. 'Ah! *Pride and Prejudice* by Jane Austen. Even I love reading her books.'

'*Pride and Prejudice* is one of my favourite novels. I reread it often especially for the Darcy vs Elizabeth encounters.' Mihir's heart is racing.

'Shall I tell you something if you don't mind?' Jyoti says with a mixture of shyness and mischief. Mihir finds her looking just beautiful with this expression on her face.

'Sure,' Mihir says clearing his throat, apprehending something discomfiting coming from Jyoti.

'The way you would run away on seeing me often reminded me of Mr Darcy,' Jyoti says, her heart beating because of the 'Mihir vs Jyoti' coming from the 'Darcy vs Elizabeth'.

'No way! I can never be that rude and condescending, that too to someone like you who is so…' Mihir's courage is overtaken by his shyness again.

'Your eyes definitely defied that impression. That's why I…' Jyoti too can't speak because of her amplifying shyness, the blush on her face saying it all.

Mihir pauses, meditating to gather his burning desire. He reclines against the wall and Jyoti senses the unease. Silence whips up their passion and speech comes to the rescue.

'Let me see the other books,' Jyoti concentrates on the books. 'Oh! Albert Camus!' She takes the book and looks at Mihir. Like a fetish, Albert Camus instantly reminds them both of that fated passionate hug and desire, making their bodies numb and taut. They move towards each other and hug each other tightly again and remain locked in a feverish spell. The pulasating passion of that drawing-room hug rises to fever pitch. From there they both move as one to the bed. As soon as they sit down Jyoti loosens herself from the hug but just enough to let Mihir look into her eyes. She is in frenzied anticipation. Mihir understands her silence and hesitatingly kisses her lips. Jyoti keeps her eyes closed but moves her head forward to convey her surrender. In that moment Mihir thinks of how girls have a penchant for the language of silence and they leave the role of the aggressor to the boys; probably this is the law of desire that Jyoti too is following, despite being vocally frank in conveying her fondness for him.

It is a heavily curtained room. The sun filters through the gaps to cast a haze of translucence and the stillness of noon heightens the pair's sense of being alone.

As soon as Mihir kisses her again they are both catapulted into a frenzied tumult of passion. They are both captivated by each others' bodies. Mihir's lips and hands are frantically exploring her body, traversing the mounds, curves and depths, to experience it in its sublime geometry all at once, while Jyoti is vigorously tossing and turning in a state of wild elation. They are trying to capture the sensations they have only imagined. The entire endeavour is bestowed with a sublime effortlessness. All their pent-up passion finds a physical outlet, leaving both of them flushed with ecstasy.

Their passion spent, the pair disengage from each other and lie side by side on the bed. Jyoti covers them with a blanket to enhance the cosiness. They are both silent, shocked beyond words. They feel enveloped in a loud lull.

Mihir's guilt has risen yet again and he thinks, 'I was apprehensive of even responding to Jyoti lest I get hijacked off my path to ambition. Uday counselled me to just experience the desire without sinking into the senti hanky-panky. Now look how I have cast myself so deep into desire, that too when my CS is just in the doldrums. This desire germinated under the excuse of her father's death. She was so sad that day and my unexpected arrival helped her recover. Can I walk away from this with no emotional baggage? Sandeep has already been pushed by his love on to a path of compromise. What if that happens to me?'

Jyoti is satiated and shining, like a pink rose under the wintry sun. And why shouldn't she be? Her desire found its outlet through its muse! But then her ecstasy is transient. No matter how ecstatic the feeling is, the lack of legitimacy in the relationship breeds guilt. But desire and guilt are the eternal bedfellows and they coexist pretty cosily.

~

Sense of Holocaust

Their silence lasts for some time. Their initial journey on the path of desire is inherently bumpy and so both of them are slightly uneasy.

'It's quite late,' Jyoti breaks the silence.

'I hope it isn't a problem and that your family will not be waiting.'

Mihir and Jyoti get back to normal and shy away from each other. Mihir drops Jyoti off at the bus stand. They are still gripped by the experience they have just shared without thinking of the future. 'When do we meet again? What is the fate of this relation?' They have managed their association after the lovemaking during their travel to Batra with the bare minimum speech.

With Jyoti gone, CS races in and eclipses everything else. With the third attempt and a change in the optional, CS rampages Mihir with fury. Prof. Sharma helps to control the fury. Mihir spends a few days reorganizing himself and his CS material. Finally he gets to Prof. Sharma's house. Having come out of the loud hustle and bustle of MN, Mihir is a bit frightened of the quiet of the house peopled only by two elderly persons. He has hardly settled in when Prof. Sharma calls him down.

'Take this. It is Karl Marx. We will begin with "thinkers". It is the most important part of Sociology and we will discuss it tomorrow afternoon.' Mihir is puzzled looking at the notebook of a hundred-odd pages and confused as to how he will finish it by the next day. Prof. Sharma senses Mihir's anxiety.

'Son, discipline is required to make up for the deficiency of time. I hope you can manage your coming prelims without bothering much,' Prof. Sharma encourages Mihir. Mihir gets to his room and begins with dialectical materialism and he finds his reading instantly interesting. Prof. Sharma asks his cook to take Mihir's dinner upstairs. Mihir's continuous impassioned spell goes on till the wee hours of the morning. Prof. Sharma is very optimistic about Mihir. Even in JNU he had a knack of picking up the promising few from the university and grooming them. He was a passionate teacher who revelled in dispensing his encyclopaedic knowledge. Mihir is glad to have gotten rid of the apes and landed in the world of humans. 'Capitalism, Division of Labour, Dehumanization, Dictatorship of Proletariat…' Mihir is finding it pretty absorbing. He finishes the notes end to end, having revisited the portions and feels reasonably quipped to face Prof. Sharma. Mihir is asked questions on the concepts of Karl Marx and he answers them all to Prof. Sharma's satisfaction.

At the end, Prof. Sharma asks, 'How do you perceive the significance of Karl Marx in modern civilization?'

'Sir, the capitalist order emerging from Adam Smith's advocacy of markets was critiqued and ultimately a new socio-political order, communism, was born, based upon the philosophy of Marx. But Marx contributed much more. While it is said that without criticism one turns blind to flaws and doesn't improve, I think the critique of Marxism ultimately proved to be the reason for the birth of an ennobled capitalist order in the world.'

'I think you will do better in Socio. It demands intelligently inserting your perspective while remaining within the scope of the question. For that matter, in the humanities in general one must do that,' Prof. Sharma says with a voice of experience.

In a matter of ten days Mihir has prepped to get introduced to Socio. He proves to be equal to the task and finds it all interesting. Even when he leaves the professor's place to brush up for his prelims, he is assigned Socio homework to be completed with the caveat that he would be tested in the professor's special way.

The prelims end with a positive impression on Mihir's mind. He has been catapulted into a frenzied endeavour by the inspirational guidance of Prof. Sharma, who not only taught him Sociology but also taught him how to approach History. Mihir's intrinsic gift for lateral thinking and connecting things to conjure up the total concept aroused Prof. Sharma's fervour.

Suresh and Mihir have become friends and have made each other's lives easier. Batra is still a haunt for Mihir whenever he needs a change and for a break from CS. There, he still feels connected to his old trio, driving him nostalgic. Movie is the perfect recipe to concoct the soma of oblivion when one wants respite from any discomfiture.

Mains have come close again, bringing up the same old anxiety. Mihir has a lot of thoughts in his mind, mainly, 'What if I fail now? Can it be a fight to the finish?' After the exams

Mihir meets Prof. Sharma who okays his performance but also reprimands Mihir for his penchant to attempt abstruse questions. However, learning from his past and Prof. Sharma's counsel, he had tried to resist his temptation to devote excessive time to the initial questions but still couldn't properly sum up the last questions of two papers. No matter how passionate you are about the subject, finishing exams gives one a sense of relief. However, no sooner than the relief started sinking in the mains result begins hounding him.

After the exams, he meets Sandeep and speaks to Uday on the phone but his anxious anticipation is not reciprocated by either of them. Sandeep is satisfied with his paper and Uday says it was inferior to his previous attempt, but he sounded detached. He tells Mihir about his plans to set up an IT venture in partnership with one of his schoolmates for which he is contemplating a one-year diploma in Computers. His tryst with Uday and Sandeep makes Mihir think, 'Ah! How our group has changed as they have moved away. The birds of different feathers are now flocking to different destinations.' He thinks of Jyoti again but diverts his mind. 'Now if I continue with her without a sense of commitment I will not be able to handle the guilt. So far she has also not asked for any commitment since she knows my inherently hesitant disposition and my commitment to my family, but what if she does ask for something or if I drown in my emotions? I should proceed only when I am ready to commit, which I am not. I want my parents to take my decisions because I want them to feel fulfilled.' For days together he remains in Delhi, struggling with his thoughts about Jyoti. Suresh has gone to Patna expecting a call for interview like his last two attempts. Mihir decides to meet his parents as he waits for the result.

His father is happy to hear his version of his mains. He has spoken to Prof. Sharma and is pretty hopeful. Mihir is scared of meeting his parents, especially as his father is now even happier because of Prof. Sharma. Mihir thinks, 'Hopes can be so scary! What if I fumble again? More the wind, louder the burst.' Just before his results, he returns to Delhi because he wants to find out how he's done instantly.

He is at Batra with Suresh and the same bustle of the motorbikes and the waiting happens again. Mihir's heart is pounding. He closes his eyes, praying in his mind to Lord Shiva. After a while, he opens his eyes and sees Suresh animatedly talking to a boy on the bike. Before he can think of anything else he sees Suresh charging triumphantly towards him and his mind says, 'I am through. Otherwise Suresh wouldn't be so elated even if he alone got through. He is not that insensitive.'

'You are through! Congratulations!' Suresh shakes Mihir's hand. He is also through but he doesn't mention it.

Mihir remains silent for a second, shaking off the hangover of the hell he has been in. He then abruptly starts running and shouting, 'Suresh, I am going to the phone booth. I have to tell Prof. Sharma and my parents.' Mihir's voice gets feebler as he continues his run through his words; he reaches the booth in a flash, in a single breath. He thinks, 'Such power in one breath! My body might have run but my heart provided the impetus.' Mihir finds it difficult to dial the phone as the receiver keeps slipping from his hand due to the rush of excitement in the body. He is trying to catch his breath.

'Sir, I am through. Thank you so much. But for you I wouldn't...'

'Son, I have no illusions. All the soldiers under one general are not the same. I only showed you to yourself,' Prof. Sharma interrupts Mihir before he adequately expresses his gratitude. 'Now the interview should be your strong point. You speak well and think analytically. I am sure you will do well.'

'Thank you, Sir. I will come to your place tomorrow,' Mihir says. In his head, 'Oh! This shyness even comes in the way of me expressing my gratitude. Why couldn't I tell him it was he who induced in me the self-belief that lends potency to karma; that I lost my first attempt because of a lack of faith in myself, looking out for some universal method to prepare. I got through now because of the confidence he gave me.'

Mihir then calls his father.

'Papa, I am through!' Mihir sounds relieved.

'Where are you? Come, come! Mihir made it through his mains. Well done, son. I should thank Prof. Sharma,' Mihir's father tells his mother the news, his words staggering with Soma.

'Now don't leave any stone unturned for your interview. Coaching and everything included, you need to put in your best.'

'I won't need coaching but I will get enrolled for Bajirao's mock interviews.'

'Okay. Now talk to your mother and sister.'

As soon as Mihir finishes talking to his family he thinks of Uday and Sandeep. Uday is not at home and his mother informs Mihir that he didn't make it through mains, dashing Mihir's hopes of seeing the trio appearing in the interview together. He decided to go to Sandeep but thinks, 'At least he will be around to share my joy. But what if he too... How will I face him? Two days back when he came to me he didn't sound too worried about his mains results.'

'So did you tell everyone? I will tell my family only when I am finally through. Since it's my third mains they won't be too happy,' Suresh tells Mihir.

'Yes I told my family. Now I feel like seeing Sandeep. I will go to Gwyer Hall to confirm his result.'

'Let me come with you. I'll meet one of my friends there.'

Mihir and Suresh head to the bus stand and run into Suresh's Gwyer Hall friend who tells them that only three from Gwyer Hall got through and Sandeep is not one of them. Mihir's excitement dims. They decide to eat at a restaurant in Kingsway Camp. Mihir has decided to treat Suresh. Suresh looks around frantically, wanting to share his results; when successful, you want others to know to get happy. Mihir too shares his emotions but in his typical subdued and sublimated manner.

Mihir wakes up the next day and the new day gives him a new feeling, an anticipation of the CS interview. 'Sitagarh, friends, Prof. Sharma, finally getting anchored and that too as a civil servant...' Mihir is lying comatose under this spell of revelry. He wakes up and starts planning his interview in his mind, rummaging through the newspapers, revising mains GS and more. Mihir feels himself more in control of his interview than he ever was for his mains. His oratorical skill is buoying him up. He meets Prof. Sharma who advises him to reread the introductory textbook on Sociology and E.H. Carr's *What is History*. He explains to Mihir to work strategically on his profile as conveyed by the form he has filled.

Mihir falls into a new rhythm of interview preparations. He misses the group study that helped with the previous exams and a memory of the trio emerges. Suresh, though friendly, is not one to be paired with for group study. He is in awe of Mihir's

English proficiency and deprecates himself as, '*Hum Hindi wale.*' In these times Mihir remembers Ajit. Thus Suresh and Mihir carry on with their independent preparations while occasionally meeting at Batra for food or a movie.

A few days before the interview they start talking on their way to Batra.

'They are saying that this time there are two new Boards for the interview. The Chairmen and new Boards go for average marking,' Suresh says.

'But how do they know that?'

'From experience. Many in such Boards have scored average despite a good performance. Hence the inference.'

'In that case, the reverse also could happen. You may benefit from average marking. Don't be anxious about 60 anymore,' Mihir tells Suresh.

'Maybe, but that is only if I get either of them. Then again, what if I get someone who mocks Hindi wale?' Suresh sounds concerned.

'But do you really believe in such hearsay? Are they sure there are no exceptions to these? I feel perception is different from reality. I know of a few Hindi chaps scoring reasonably well,' Mihir assures Suresh.

While they continue talking about the interview, Mihir thinks, 'Now I will not be perturbed by this kind of hearsay. The mains have taught me that.'

Finally the day of the interview arrives. Suresh has been kind enough to arrange his cousin's car for Mihir. Suresh's interview is two days later.

Mihir enters the UPSC premises and picks out his slip. He gets one of the two new Boards and he meditates for a moment to ignore his anxiety. He is shown into the hall and finds candidates either absorbed in newspapers or meditating. Mihir is feeling less anxious than he felt during his mains till he gets the call to go inside. As soon as he sits on the chair, he is transported into a 'sucked-in-squeezed-out' world. Once it is done, Mihir feels okay about his interview, notwithstanding the two unanswered questions and the occasional eclipses of his voice out of nervousness. The CS judges give the verdict, '180–195.' Prof. Sharma is also satisfied with the interview, so much so that Mihir thinks, 'What if I end up letting him down!'

Suresh gets a real monster for his interview and feels slain even before going into the battlefield. He emerges feeling okay by his standards but Mihir is sceptical because of his 'Bihari Hindi'.

'What if I flunk again! I have decided not to quit before exhausting my attempts. They have given me seven. Otherwise Papa's business is waiting for me,' Suresh often says when he gets desperate. His words often leave Mihir thinking, 'How easy for him to pursue CS without the baggage of insecurity; he is not opening another door, which is understandable, but on what confidence did I shut all the other doors?'

An optimistic Mihir leaves for Sitagarh to brave the hopes sheltering in his home.

The D day arrives and the evening radio announces that the results have been declared. Mihir does not tell anyone at home and calls Suresh in Delhi for the results. After a long wait the phone rings.

'What? Are you sure? Make sure there is no mistake,' Mihir's comment draws everyone in the house to him. Everyone interprets his words as him not making it. His family is deflated.

Mihir flings himself on the sofa with a balloon-bursting thud and is too shocked to cry. Parents, Sitagarh, Faizpur, friends, Prof. Sharma...everything comes crashing down.

~

The Last Chance

The train chugs off from the platform. Mihir is at the footboard, looking with pensive eyes at his father whose eyes are wet with withheld tears. The thought of 'How can I cry before my son?' is stopping the tears from streaming out. He is finding it tough to withstand the miseries of his son. Since the results of the third attempt, Mihir and his father have not exchanged a syllable on CS; silence tells it all, speech slices the heart. Father and son know not only what each one is thinking but may think as well; the empathy is absolute. Mihir's mother is frazzled but cannot tell her son that maybe his choice was wrong. Somehow she is remorseful about not impeding the 'shut all the other doors' campaign of the father-son duo for CS.

Mihir tries to gauge his father's thoughts. 'I had full faith in my son's abilities and not without reason but destiny is willing otherwise. I should have paid heed to his mother's sane advice about having a backup. I just wanted to see him happy, unfettered by the mundane realities of life. Even my colleagues advised that and their sons are now well settled with good banking and private-sector jobs. Only my son is left behind. Now the people of Sitagarh will mock the "like father, like son" adage that used to give me pride. But I have dealt with a lot in my life. I can take this too. But my son? For him it was not just a career option, but a matter of pride. His tender self will wilt under this impregnable despair. He is already a bit melancholic in his disposition. But I am also to be blamed for being party to his blind passion. I should have resisted the temptation of controlling his destiny with karma; success is a blend of the two.'

As soon as Mihir somehow manages to deposit himself on the upper berth, he immediately bursts into profuse tears, his mind hushing his cries; at times social habits guard you against going crazy. His mind says, 'I have failed my parents, more so my father. I have failed myself. Many of lesser ability have made it through but why not me?

'Oh Shiva, if you don't want to bless me with success, at least get me out of this quagmire of false hope and plant me on some other course in life; this addiction is just pathological. I have seen the lifeless creatures loitering the streets of MN. All of my friends are somewhere. What is my destiny? Bless me with peace of mind.

'If you don't want to help me, I will help myself. It was probably because of my extraneous deficiencies like poor time management and illegible handwriting in the later part of the papers, leaving the paper incomplete, not adhering to word limit, relying more on perceptions than facts while writing my answers, etc. There is still space left to improve my karma so I will wait before I curse my destiny. Anyway I have shut all my doors and am beyond trying for a new option so my fourth attempt is the fait accompli. So let me experience the thrill of handling this last attempt with a "nothing to lose" elan, an adventure untainted with fear.

'Oh! I am again falling into this trap of false hopes. I still don't have a life beyond a barren last attempt. Standing on the edge of the cliff, I still hope to scale the summit. Okay let me get rid of the hopes and stick to karma without bothering about my destiny.'

He is frantically scribbling in his diary, 'The elixir of life either in the form of hope or in the form of karma is distilled through the tribute of tears to Lord Shiva.'

Mihir is lulled into an quietude after the catharsis, just thinking how Lord Shiva has been there both ways, when he begged Him for success, and also when he was angry with Him and resolved to gather back his karma to challenge His verdict if it was 'No'. He remembers Uday saying, 'God has such fun since believers and non-believers both remember Him in equal measure.' The whiff of nostalgia embalms his mind and he falls asleep.

Mihir reaches Delhi. He confirms whether he will get a last attempt. Even the most pessimistic assessment keeps him in the safe zone. Mihir has not gone to Prof. Sharma. He is shy and ashamed at letting him down. But he cannot vanish altogether because his CS material is at the professor's house.

He calls Prof. Sharma the next morning.

'Sir…' Mihir is speechless.

'So it didn't happen? I know. Your father told me. So what next?' Prof. Sharma asks.

'I am clueless…' Mihir replies.

'Just answer my questions. Are you ready to turn militant?' Prof. Sharma asks.

'Yes.' Mihir knows there is no other answer.

'Do you think your weapons can be sharpened further?'

'Yes,' Mihir agrees.

'Then come now. You are fit enough.'

'But Sir…' Prof. Sharma cuts the line with a 'militant' click, instantly snapping Mihir's further slide into his soggy despair; at times sounds are more unequivocal than words.

Mihir thinks, 'Fighting is in my fate anyway. Then why not under the inspirational aura of Prof. Sharma which will help me manage my despair?'

The next day Mihir leaves for Prof. Sharma's place.

'Come in. The door is open,' Mihir hears the professor's voice from the window.

As soon as Mihir sits down, Prof. Sharma says, 'I am sure you must have done well in the interview. I can get you better at Sociology. You agree that your weapons need sharpening...'

Mihir tries to hesitantly explain his thoughts from the train, struggling for his speech through the rush of emotions.

'Sorry, militants don't mew, they roar. If you continue this, you can leave right now,' Prof. Sharma is irritated.

'Sir, I feel like there are people who can't strike a chemistry with CS. I have seen many good people getting rejected. It is beyond an intelligence-diligence equation.' Mihir knows Prof. Sharma is giving him the shock treatment by telling him to leave.

'My dear son! In life certain chemistries have to be concocted. Just pay heed to experience, otherwise by the time you earn it, it will be too late.' Prof. Sharma softens a little. 'You know pretty much everything. Just practise writing and make things precise by blending the right facts in your answers.

I will be disappointed if you don't make it. Bureaucracy needs original thought.'

'I will try. I don't have any other options anyway.'

'Not having other options is sometimes the best way to attain single-mindedness. This time, spend more time here. I am eager to know your marks.' Prof. Sharma tries cheering Mihir up.

Mihir tries to resume his studies but his heart won't listen to his mind and he is too tired. He knows that getting through the prelims is a status quo. He gets through his mains preparations even though rhythm fails him. The marksheet is not a surprise and the marks are not proportional to his expectations. He gets more in Sociology than History. His interview brings some cheer—195, which is good by all standards. Prof. Sharma is elated at his correct prediction.

'I told you, not everything is so unpredictable. Your essay is very good, so is your expression, both written and oral.' Prof. Sharma studies the marksheet.

Mihir thinks, 'What I exert upon the least again pays the better dividend. My innate qualities always pay me. I am a creature of the flow. My mind and my heart are sapped by discipline.'

His wading improves to swimming but Mihir is dispassionate. He turns into a strange melee of the extremes; optimism–pessimism, buoyancy–deflation, faith–doubt. His emotions vary but never reach excitement. It is like some weight planted atop the spring. Even the approaching mains don't seem to change his feelings. His heart doesn't beat as wildly as earlier and the butterflies don't flutter in his stomach. He feels inert. It's like his nerves are so tired that they are beyond excitement. He wonders if his behaviour is about ease or life teaching him detachment; if the detachment entails this flatness in life, Krishna was not exciting at all in preaching detached attachment, or was he getting him wrong? He wonders if this is Sandeep's Buddhist diminishing of desire—if so Sandeep's Buddha is pretty boring.

As Mihir is studying at Prof. Sharma's, Mrs Sharma enters the room.

'I hope you are comfortable,' she says.

'Yes Aunty. Thank you for all this...' Mihir says, getting up from bed.

'Study well, son. He was very upset because he felt you had pinned his hopes on him but...'

'No, no. It is only because of him that I switched to Sociology and scored reasonably well. It's I who is lacking somewhere.'

'Actually, let me tell you something. He also wrote the civil services exams but couldn't make it. Seeing you passionately chase your dream has made him nostalgic and he is emotionally entangled in your CS. He says that if you get through, he will feel fulfilled,' Mrs Sharma explains.

Mihir thinks, 'Man's cravings for excitement can be dormant but they never die. Till the other day I didn't even know these people and now a part of our worlds have got instantly connected.'

Mihir and Prof. Sharma work on many things including Mihir's handwriting. Mihir keeps shuttling between his MN house and Prof. Sharma's before finally shifting to MN for his mains.

He finishes his last paper, Socio-II. He has not found anything unusual about his papers. Prof. Sharma is also satisfied except for a few issues here and there, like his selection of questions. He has often said, 'Never attempt a question without being sure what is being asked.' But somehow Mihir derives a kick from attempting a tricky question.

The next day he slips on the stairs and fractures his hand. He is in deep pain. Suresh helps in getting it plastered. Suresh becomes closer to Mihir and assists him in all his tasks.

Mihir leaves for Sitagarh in a state of frozen turmoil. He is scared of exploring his mind right now, a journey he otherwise loves to undertake.

The whistle of the train leaving the station creates a vacuum in his heart. He is going back to Sitagarh empty-handed with nothing in his future. His parents, his foolishness at not having options, society's ridicule... everything together is driving him crazy. He feels like killing himself but knows his parents will not be able to bear it. He remembers Durkheim from Socio, 'A man commits suicide when anomie sets in, a total disconnect from his surroundings.' He thinks, 'I am still connected to my parents and myself. If death comes on its own, do I want to die?' The confusion deepens in his mind which, not knowing anything beyond, ultimately gets frozen on Shiva for the soma of sanity. Mind lands on the thought, 'I may not have succeeded in the civil services but I shouldn't doubt my intrinsic abilities. I can make a living out of my writing. But being different means a grim struggle, which saps the senses and consumes the youth. Oh! If only I could forget everything and be a happy Buddhist, shorn of desire, or if this world could get eclipsed in a flash and start anew!' Exhausted by all this thinking, his mind goes into a stupor; mind snatches the respite for itself. The journey for Mihir is like hide-and-seek with the monster his consciousness brings into being in myriad forms.

His stay at home is ruled by silence, everyone deciphering each other's hearts unequivocally. Mihir doesn't meet his acquaintances since society looks monstrous to him. This time he has decided to hear his results at Sitagarh, scared of being alone. These days his mind is frequently assaulted by rationality. He thinks, 'Only parents can give succour to their failed child. God is the child of man, created by one's mind to be tapped for soma when in such distress. Like a child He is kept close in all circumstances; love, scold, hate...whatever you do He is there with you. Oh! Rationality is so tormenting, it spoils the cosy cocoons so meticulously woven by the heart!' The train of Mihir's thoughts continues, 'God's help is neither visible nor knowable; when we succeed we ascribe it to God's grace. When we fail and try to ascribe it to God, they condemn you, calling you a fatalist; God escapes scot-free.'

The situation growing scarier, astrology jumps in.

'I know of a very knowledgeable Panditji. People vouch for the accuracy of his predictions. He predicted that Mrs Sinha's son would be a doctor and it happened. Maybe we should consult him,' Mihir's mother says.

'I don't believe in these things. Who can understand God's world? It is not feasible to foretell man's future.' Mihir's father brushes her proposal aside.

'What proof do you have that it is farce? You always brush aside these things by calling them superstitions,' his mother counters.

'You are pushing a young rational boy into this. Who can believe that the planets control man's life?' His father is charged up.

'And can you prove it doesn't happen? Man has seen the planets, but what about God? He is unseen yet believed in even by the intellectuals like you. It is human belief which makes a stone God,' his mother says. 'Only the mind cannot run this world; the heart is needed too.'

'Okay, no more arguing. You can take him along.' Mihir's father yields.

Mihir finds the exit of karma from the scene strangely comforting. He thinks, 'I have now exhausted my efforts, and now it is the turn of destiny to deliver.'

Mihir's father has also accompanied them to the Panditji. 'Man shouldn't always mitigate his miseries. Managing them is equally important.'

Mihir is amused at seeing his life turned into a matter of mathematics. 'The entire universe has been squeezed into these geometrical squares and diamonds. It's like man's future is such a simple calculation. What a fool I have been thus far, groping hopelessly confused in the blind alleys of esoteric karma and destiny!' Mihir is waiting for the verdict.

'If he gives a negative verdict, can I leave my CS interview if I am through my mains? No.'

'Rahu at this wrong place is playing some mischief. Saturn also is ferocious but Jupiter, his lord, will finally come to dominate them. Just make him wear a horseshoe to please Saturn and a garnet ring to counter Rahu. He will get a very prestigious government job,' Panditji pronounces smugly.

Mihir thinks, 'What did man do to please Rahu and Saturn when there was no iron to make a horseshoe and no garnets? When Vishnu's chakra wasn't capable of slaying a serpent and instead could only cut it into two, leaving it to hiss with Rahu as the head and Ketu as the tail, what can a mundane garnet do to fix the issues?'

The hangover of the soma offered by Panditji dispels some fear of the demon, but it stays put to keep hounding Mihir. The house simmers with unease.

'The radio has announced that the mains results are out. Let me call Deven and check,' Mihir tells his mother who is lying down.

'Hmm,' his mother says, extremely scared. His father has overheard him and his sisters also feel a change.

'What has to happen will happen. No one can challenge destiny,' his father says, but his words do not match his expression.

The Panditji has vanished from the scene.

A hush settles on the house.

'How long will it take?' Mihir's father asks, sitting on the sofa.

'You know how fast it is,' Mihir replies.

After an hour the phone rings. The ring of the phone has never seemed this eerie. Everyone freezes. Mihir answers and in a split second drops it. 'Got through.' The tautness in the air instantly dissolves. But this time Mihir's hope is haunted with the thought 'This is the last chance; what if I finally don't make it?' The excitement of getting through mains eludes him.

Mihir gets ready to leave for Delhi. He is in two minds about going back but one has to live no matter what. The house is back to its uneasy silence. His father is at the platform and Mihir is on the upper berth of the train, evoking a sense of déjà vu.

This time Mihir doesn't take Bajirao's mock personality test. The last time their assessment of 165 was converted into

195 and personality cannot be taught the rapid fire way. One good thing about his last interview was that his anxiety didn't become a handicap for him.

Suresh has made it through his mains for the fourth time. For Mihir Suresh's company is soma but for Suresh it is prana. Mihir's thinking and speaking draws Suresh in. They go through the motions of studying for the interview by reading the newspapers and catching up on current affairs. But all this is performed like a ritual, shorn of the thrill of anticipation. This sense of detachment is so tormenting for them. Probably the rules of dharma militate against the natural design of man.

'My last three attempts have been 60, 60, 60. I didn't even hit three digits. Being a Hindi-medium guy, I lose heart before the interview itself. The mock interviews also don't help much because even they treat us Hindi speakers with contempt. I once even flunked my qualifying English and lost my first mains. This English is sort of an unending horror show,' Suresh vents out his frustration to Mihir.

Suresh's words send a disturbing streak of smugness in Mihir. 'I don't have any issue with my English.' Suresh's Hindi also has a heavy dose of Bhojpuri and he wonders, 'Can he really surmount his handicap?' As usual before the answer springs up, Mihir ejects himself from the discomfiture.

'Had I got even a 140–45, I would have been somewhere high up with the advantage of the OBC factor,' Suresh says and Mihir wonders, 'He manages to score higher than me in the mains? Cramming Hindi grammar is serving him well. He even learns his Stats in GS-I through memorizing. Zeal can make you do anything.'

'I would suggest that you don't work on your interview but

your Hindi. What matters is to speak the language correctly,' Mihir advises.

'How come you speak Hindi so well despite living in Bihar?' Suresh asks Mihir enviously.

'I will definitely help you practise speaking in Hindi.' Mihir offers his help.

Thus the run-up to the personality test has been eased by Suresh's company, occasional visits to Prof. Sharma, scribbling of verses in a fit of creativity and strolls to Batra that remind him of his friends, with Jyoti as a background score.

Mihir is helping Suresh practise. 'History repeats itself; do you agree?' Mihir asks him the question Prof. Sharma had asked him.

Suresh gathers himself and begins in Hindi, '*Main pichale teen varshon se mains pass karta aaya hoon lekin interview mein hamesha shaatt number milta hai aur main shafal naheen ho pata hoon. Mujhe doosre saal ke baad aisa ehshas hua ki itihas apne aap ko dohrata hai.*'

Mihir counsels, 'You tend to pronounce "sh" instead of "sa" in certain words, like "ehshas" is actually "eh-saas" and "shafal" is "safal". Also you have to practise repeating certain words many times so that the tongue gets used to the twists they demand. About your answer, you should have imported some genuine historical examples to explain it. History is not yesterday and not mundane.' Mihir is happy to be helping Suresh and is also a bit smug himself. He has even forgotten his own interview. Suresh helps Mihir by recording his interview for him to listen to it later. Whenever Mihir stays with Suresh, he is reminded of the boy in DU who was running around screaming, 'My roommate who flies to his place will get covered under the

Mandal Commission.'

Mihir's interview is tomorrow and Suresh's is today. He is happy with his performance and says he didn't falter as much this time. Mihir feels himself getting nudged out of his inertness, the day passing with emotions wrestling with each other, 'Let it pass off quick; if only this world could get eclipsed.' In the night his blazing mind thinks before he sleeps, 'Tomorrow my tryst with CS ends. It is either here or nowhere.' He is so worried and overwhelmed that he goes to the bathroom feeling like vomiting but is unable to. He gets back to bed but can't sleep. The ticking watch and the humming fan never sounded so ominously horrific; sort of like a countdown to the guillotine. However, Mihir has not forgotten to fortify himself with the tabeez, given by his mother's Panditji.

Suresh accompanies Mihir to UPSC, arranging for his cousin's car.

'I hope you get some monster who awards either 60 or 200 plus,' Suresh says with a smile. 'I know you will get what you deserve.'

Mihir goes in and takes his slip. It turns out Suresh was right. Mihir enters the waiting hall and sees a hysterical girl screaming out some questions to the candidates while another boy is almost fainting and being helped by a girl. He waits in the corridor, trying to invoke his Shiva for some tranquillity. 'Many are miserable, it's not only me,' Mihir thinks. At times the knowledge of others' miseries affords some ease.

It is now Mihir's turn.

'I have been screwed,' a boy comes out mumbling. Mihir closes in on him before going inside the room.

'I am Manavendra. The Chairman virtually packed me off

by saying I have already pocketed IPS and so why am I trying again. He didn't take any interest in me. I was in his Board last year also and he gave me a 90. I still managed because of my written score.' Mihir is gripped by the thought that he is nowhere in the services and so cannot be empathetic.

Mihir is ushered in but can't see the Chairman in the room. Then he turns around and sees him drinking water. In response to his greeting, Mihir is gestured to take his seat. He feels apprehensive as sitting down would mean turning his back to the Chairman. He sits facing slightly sideways to acknowledge the presence of the Chairman standing behind. The Chairman then sits down in his chair and looks at Mihir's profile. The pause has eclipsed Mihir's mind and all his thoughts have vanished. From here Mihir is not conscious of how he will act or what he will say. He feels like prey to the panelists.

'You have indicated that yoga is your hobby. Do you have any other interests?' the Chairman begins.

'I like watching cricket and Hindi movies.'

'Movies? Okay, any particular kind, or by any particular director or starring any particular actor?' the Chairman continues.

'I like movies directed by Gulzar and those of Amitabh Bachchan and Sanjeev Kumar.'

'Sanjeev Kumar! Why?'

'I find his acting effortless and he is truly versatile.'

'Yes that he is. Can you name the movie where he played many roles at once?'

'*Naya Din Nayi Raat*, he played nine roles in this movie,' Mihir finally feels a little comfortable.

'How do you see India in 2010?' the Chairman asks.

Mihir talks about the changing face of politics, the arrival of the coalition era with the emergence of regional parties; developments in science and technology, especially space; the liberalization and globalization of the economy, etc. The Chairman prompts him to throw light on the issues he left out, like women's issues and more. Then the interview passes on to the next member who asks a few questions on History.

The next panellist is female and she asks, 'Recently Buddha's statue was demolished in Bamiyan in Afghanistan by some fundamentalist elements. How do you view the event?'

'This is an attack by fanatics upon the ideal of secularism and is highly condemnable,' Mihir says.

'How do you perceive it?' she asks again.

'It may be perceived as an assault upon the value of non-violence by violence. Buddha remains one of the first to preach non-violence to the world,' he tries again.

'Any other interpretation? How do you place the event?' she asks again with a gentle smile.

'It's like encouraging parochialism with regard to ideology, ideals and intellect. It could convey the message that the statue of Budhha, an Indian, can't exist in Afghanistan because it is now a separate Islamic country. It is like geography determining the journey of ideas and knowledge, which is ridiculous,' Mihir answers again without getting perturbed by the repetition of the question. He is unable to sense that it might be because his answer is not convincing enough.

'Any other way you can see it?' she prompts again.

'Well...it can also be seen as religion being brought into the realm of politics and international relations in a world which is veering towards liberalization and globalization and where the economy and well-being of nations are the deciding factors in international diplomacy. For example, China and the US entering trade facilitation relations even though they otherwise don't have cordial relations because of ideological considerations.'

'Any other way you can see it?' the lady is dangerously centred on her question. Mihir is still not conscious of what is happening and his mind is obsessed with inventing new logic in response.

'It may be seen as a signal to the world of the growing virulence of Islamic fundamentalism and even India has to guard itself as Afghanistan is our neighbour,' Mihir replies, still calm.

Finally the lady spares him and the next member takes over. The lady is still smiling at him and Mihir can't decipher the mystery of the repeated questions on the Bamiyan Buddha.

For a split second Sandeep's Buddha crosses his mind.

'You mentioned a while back about China and the US striking economic relations. These days the world is turning euphoric about the economic boom in China. India is being prompted to follow China as a controlled communist polity with a capitalist economy on a high growth path or a democracy with average growth. What will you choose?'

'Always democracy with average growth. Freedom of expression is invaluable. Even the hungry hanker for a voice. Individuality shouldn't be sacrificed at the altar of the state and a balance between order and freedom should be the aim. Moreover, even a democracy can put itself on a high growth path, like the US. India is taking liberalizing measures to put itself on a path of sustained higher economic growth,' despite his nervousness, Mihir is happy with his answer.

The mantle for the mastication has passed on to the last member after two-three more questions.

'Your profile says you have stayed in Bihar. These days Bihar is in the news for all the wrong reasons, like the animal husbandry corruption case. We notice that people and media are demanding the resignation of political leaders even before the final verdict is out on the plea that such legal processes take too long. Is this trend correct?'

'Sir, in politics perception is stronger than reality. People feel strongly on issues where the smoke waxes so dense that fire can just not be precluded and the general image of a political leader also decides whether he or she should be given the benefit of doubt or not. Overall, public opinion should be honoured in a democracy. Anyway in such cases, the politician can come back if not proved guilty. The sanctity of the legal process should be zealously guarded to preserve justice.' Mihir manages to strike a middle path.

'I think that's all,' the Chairman says as he looks at the other members for their consent to release the prey. The interview lasted close to an hour. Mihir leaves and when he is out, a bizarre mix of emotions stills him. Mihir thinks, 'Was it good? I think it was, except for the occasional eclipse of my expression due to nervousness.' Mihir's mind tosses up contentment for him. His tryst with CS is over and a sense of 'what next' overwhelms him. For a fleeting moment the anticipation of success tickles his heart into a thrill.

Suresh is waiting for him and he tells him about the interview with a sense of detachment. Suresh judges it highly, but no one can be an ideal judge. CS is an enigma and nobody has a clue.

Prof. Sharma is gaga over Mihir's interview. 'You don't realize that your unyielding vigour on the Buddha question may do the magic. That is what they test, your nerve. Your China answer was also pretty good and of course your natural take on your other interests. Your written was also better this time; just pray for your destiny.'

Mihir feels that Prof. Sharma has been the soma which made possible the navigation through his last attempt. 'I have heard that the fieriest of dreams gets extinguished in the darkness of despair but if someone could pull it out just when it's about to get blown out, it may survive but…' Mihir sighs.

~

The Mona Lisa Finale

Thus Mihir is on the last leg of his CS journey.

Mihir decides not to go home and so does Suresh. The two together brew soma to lubricate their path to…where?

'Shall we go to Sujeet Jha, a journalist friend of mine? He is supposed to be a good palmist and many vouch for his accuracy. He also appeared for CS thrice but couldn't make it and later did his Mass. Comm. from Times School,' Suresh proposes.

'You appear to be a keen believer in palmistry and astrology. You are already wearing three stones,' Mihir says disinterestedly.

'When survival is at stake, beliefs go for a toss.'

'You mean soma?'

'Soma?' Suresh is confused.

Mihir smiles, fondly recalling his days with the trio when they discovered somas of all possible flavours. Then he thinks of how Uday is now settled in his successful IT venture and Sandeep in his teaching assignment at DU while he is alone.

Mihir agrees to go to meet Sujeet Jha and they head to Indira Vihar.

'You just said he couldn't configure CS,' Mihir says.

'Configure?' Suresh asks.

'Yes. Configure CS by fixing the planets. They can turn gigantic planets with tiny stones on your fingers,' Mihir says mischievously.

Suresh also smiles. They get to the house and see a boy offering money.

'He takes money? I mean, is he a professional?'

'Yes, but he won't charge me. He's my friend,' Suresh is boastful like a priest is about God.

'No, it will take too long and I don't have the patience. I don't want soma from this shop.' Mihir does not enter. 'This is just a part of a parallel economy. I know how soma is needed to negotiate a bumpy ascent and so this guy has decided to trade in soma itself.'

'What is this soma that you keep speaking of? If you mean soma rasa, how is astrology that?' Suresh is confused.

Mihir thinks, 'Suresh drinks all flavours yet doesn't know what is soma. There are many like him drinking without knowing.'

Time for Mihir is crawling; the run-up to the final result appears to be unbearably long. Mihir thinks, 'Who says time is constant—the mind can make an hour of a minute and a minute of an hour; happen what may, but quickly...'

There are about ten-fifteen days left before the final judgment. Mihir is on his bed post dinner. He is pondering as usual; however, tonight it is a different house, not CS but post-CS. He writes in his diary but it is not a verse. It is a piece on Sufis in the CS world; their God, their roots, their journey, their failure, their success. In one flow he ends up writing almost five compact pages. He reads-edits-reads…to get a finished piece in a matter of less than two hours. He sleeps restfully and wakes up feeling better. He is amazed at himself. 'Am I really convinced I am not going to get through? Who is motivating me to think of life post CS? I know I will make a living out of my writing but the results are still awaited…'

'Shall we go to your friend today? It's Sunday and he may be home,' Mihir asks Suresh.

'But you were not keen before. Suddenly what happened?' Suresh is curious.

'I will tell you later. First let me meet him,' Mihir replies.

'Okay.'

They head to Suresh's friend's place again.

'What is this paper you are holding in your hands?'

'You will know when we reach there,' Mihir smiles.

'Suddenly this…' Suresh is now more curious.

They reach Sujeet's place and he is home with no one else around. Suresh introduces them to each other and niceties are exchanged. Suresh offers his palm, poised to hear a yes. Sujeet's verdict is a yes-no, more yes than no, as it happens when the client's face is right there before you. Mihir also offers his palm lest Sujeet should think that Mihir is undermining his skills to foretell.

'This time the chances are very bright. Rahu is just positioned a bit adversely to counter the solidly placed Jupiter but you are already wearing a golden sapphire to strengthen Jupiter,' Sujeet says.

'Now with hardly ten-fifteen days left, the suspense will end. I have come to you for one more purpose,' Mihir says.

'Yes…'

Mihir gives him the paper and says, 'I have written a piece of prose about our world. I want you to read it and get your editorial board to read it too. See if it can find a place on the features page of your newspaper. I want to test my writing skills.'

'Sure. In fact we keep looking for such stuff. The topic is quite interesting—Sufis in trance.' Sujeet starts reading.

'Read it in your own time. There is no hurry,' Mihir says.

'I hope it's not a problem?' Suresh double checks.

'Give me a week or so,' Sujeet says.

'Thank you. It's very helpful of you,' Mihir replies.

They disperse after their tea, back to their routine. They work themselves into birdwatching as well but are too distracted. The sparks elude them. A week has passed and Mihir and Suresh head to meet Sujeet.

'Mihir, I have started feeling jittery. The date is closer...'

'You can't do anything. That is the price for taking on the demon but somehow when getting slain seems a certainty even fear eludes you. Somehow I am not feeling jittery.' Mihir is focused on the fate of his writing and Sujeet's verdict.

They reach Sujeet's house and he is with clients.

'I was just thinking of taking a stroll to your place,' Sujeet says as they arrive.

'Anything important? Otherwise you are a busy man,' Suresh says.

'I read your article and it was superb. I got my senior editor also to read it and he was admiring it quite a bit. They are offering you a job. It's a new newspaper and they are trying to build a good team. They are looking for people for their magazine, which will be launched soon,' Sujeet is excited, and a bit smug too.

'But I have not studied the subject. How can I...'

'If you are good without that it is not a problem. They will put your article in the next Sunday feature.' Sujeet is excited.

Mihir is happy. The rejection by CS had challenged his self-esteem but he has realized that his innate talent has never failed to pay him dividends. Noorjahan, West Asia, essay scores, Prof. Sharma admiring his natural gift for lateral thinking and now his article are all falling into an exciting order. He thinks, 'If I am not destined to make it in CS and win worldly success for myself, my parents and society, and if my youth has to be consumed by a struggle for living, let it be for the realization of my passion, not just any job for survival. There are many examples of writers attaining success late in their life after a prolonged struggle. It is a fire which is not dimmed by the fire going feeble in the kitchen; heart has a penchant for fighting the hunger.' Premchand, Bimal Mitra, John Keats spring up in his mind. For a fleeting moment 'Am I again getting in the trap of hope?' crosses his mind, leaving him a bit ruffled up. He motivates himself, 'Anyway it's a matter of a few days. Let my fate be decided and I will see after that.'

As they approach Batra, they sense the familiar excitement, the same razzmatazz. Their hearts beat faster and even Mihir is excited. Suresh asks someone and it is confirmed that the final results are out.

'Don't worry. I have already given our numbers to my cousin who lives in Jor Bagh. Let me call him,' Suresh takes Mihir to the phone booth.

'He is going to UPSC right away,' says Suresh when he emerges. 'Meanwhile, we go to the Hanuman temple. He will call at my place at the landlord's number.'

They go to the temple and then get to the flat. Hardly a few minutes later, 'Suresh!' the landlady calls.

'Yes Aunty,' Suresh responds.

'Phone call. It's your brother.'

'Coming, Aunty…' Suresh and Mihir run to the phone.

Suresh picks up the phone and after a second's pause is beaming. He puts the phone down, hugs Mihir and is both crying and laughing while blabbering. '141 yours, 185 mine, 141…' Then he calms himself and responds to Aunty's curiosity.

'Come on, let's call home, let's meet friends…Batra…I am in the IAS!' Suresh is ecstatic and on Cloud Nine, repeatedly stroking his hair in a fit of excitement. 'Magic it is literally.' Suresh says and goes out.

They head to Batra, Suresh looking around for people he knows so that he can brag about becoming godly in this Sufi world.

Mihir is still stunned. He calls home.

'Hello!' It's the anxious voice of his mother.

"Through, Mummy!' Mihir says.

'He is through, he is through!'

'What is his rank?' It's his sister's voice.

'Let the rank go to hell! My son is finally somewhere. He is saved…' His mother is hysterical.

'We have to tell Papa. He just went out. Chotu! Go find him,' his sister screams.

Mihir overhears all of this and smiles to himself. He hangs up and leaves. 'Finally I am there,' ...the feeling is yet to sink into him. His inertness has still not released him.

'Babuji is jumping. As a businessman he hungered for bureaucracy. Now his own son is in. Knowing him, by now half of Patna has probably heard the news. What about you?' Suresh is still ecstatic.

'Papa is out. Mummy got hysterical. Even from here I could see my home erupt into joy,' Mihir says.

'But why are you still so downcast? Aren't you happy? I had another attempt left, but you? Your last attempt! You should be thankful to God,' Suresh says.

'Hmm... God,' Mihir smiles through the sombreness.

'You go ahead to the flat. I have to meet a few friends. Tonight the beer is on me,' Suresh says.

Mihir goes to the phone booth again to call Prof. Sharma, his godfather. When he tells his news, Mihir can hear him getting emotional, 'My dear son. Real militancy never fails to fire. I knew you had it in you but you deserved better...' he pauses.

'I will come tomorrow,' Mihir hangs up.

Mihir heads home and thinks, 'God is there either way. When I was failing, they said it is God's will and your karma and now when I have succeeded they say it is God's grace. When is it karma and when God? Is it destiny that made me get through in my last attempt? There is no sense of God's existence without a feeling of destiny. I can safely say that I was more deserving of CS than many who got through with greater ease, so where is God in my scheme of CS?'

Mihir gets home and falls on his bed, staring at the fan. He thinks, 'Just a while back, I was happy about my article being good enough to win me a joining offer. Just two hours of effort; this is the magic of the flow, this is destiny. As of now let me enter the services to experience it in all its possible hues—the ability to effect changes in others' lives, immense social prestige, the happiness of my family... I revelled in writing verses and now the Sujeet episode has ignited another dream in my head by fetching affirmation for my flair for writing.'

'Why are you lying down?' Suresh's is back.

'Nothing, just...' Mihir gets up.

'Come on. I have bought a crate of beer. We will raise a storm tonight.' Suresh drags Mihir downstairs.

'I have to go out again. I need to speak to my father,' Mihir says.

'Okay, but get back quickly. Suresh Kumar, you are in the IAS now!' Suresh is dancing.

Mihir is back after talking to his father.

'How did your father react?' Suresh pours the beer.

'He was surrounded by his friends who had arrived to wish him. He sounded ecstatic...' Mihir raises a toast to a feverishly cheering Suresh. 'But he conveyed my mother's feelings to me. "You, father and son, made a mole out of a mountain, an adventure out of a vocation. The civil services is fine but closing all doors to create this kind of uncertain existence, so edgy." I was enjoying her emotions but it's only the life of sensations which affords real ecstasy.' Mihir is already tipsy with his rapidly enthused gulps. They have decided to douse themselves in soma tonight without bothering to be trippy, revelling in the resonance of the two somas—success and beer. But the trio is constantly buzzing in his mind like a background score. 'Alas! Only if it was Uday and Sandeep with me, all of us through!' Mona Lisa is burgeoning in Mihir's heart.

'Mihir, just wait and see how tomorrow morning the boys buzz themselves to you. It is just an out-of-the-world feeling!' Suresh is drinking fast out of joy.

Mihir is in self-searching mode. The party over, he staggers to his room and falls on his bed. 'My family is high and my mother will be smug in her society. My peers will think I was bound for this. How nice it will be to go to Sitagarh now!'

The scene in his mind changes and his melancholia blazes, affording a revelatory comprehension. Mihir feels an exciting anticipation throbbing in him as another dream of being a writer has begun. 'Mona Lisa is the most attractive hue in life, always leaving something to be desired, with shades of both pain and pleasure. These pangs of pain are actually the pangs of the birth of another dream... Uday was right when he said perfect happiness is scary and any change will make you less happy. The conception of another dream after this delivery is just excitingly bizarre. I am angry for not being blessed with destiny. God, I don't know, but Lord Shiva whom I kept invoking to give me an anchor, who didn't let me falter from the CS path? Who made my father support me in my romantic dream of CS? What if the trio were not there to afford me soma to lubricate the initial rigour of the journey? Who made me meet Prof. Sharma? What if I had fractured my wrist again just a day before? Who didn't let me flounder in my last prelims despite my lack of confidence in my performance in the penultimate attempt? Who was the one I challenged in my moments of failure to resolve my karma? Was it Lord Shiva or my conception of soma or... Travelling is better than arriving. Lord Shiva, just be kind to me and keep blessing me with dreams which brew an eternal soma, and keep giving me karma, as karma is the only means to test my destiny...' Mihir bursts into tears as the mixed glow of catharsis lights in him.

~

The Writer Speaks

Dear Readers,

When I started this journey into the past to tell you the story of the pursuit of my fiery ambition of getting into the civil services, I wished to transport you all back at the same Green Park flat from where this journey took off. I was not sure about how well the snapshots and the vignettes at my command then will come to serve me in melting into the time gone by and the words that will emerge to describe it. But as I went deeper into the past, not only did they flow to their full potential, but also new memories kept rising from the deeper recesses of my mind to illuminate the past in its finest nuances. Thus, I have decided to break the journey into two parts and, as of now, to leave you at Mihir reaching his cherished destination—civil services. So Ruchi's advice to narrate how the cherished destination got converted into a trap, that I mentioned at the outset, remains uncomplied with. This will be told in the next leg of the journey extending from the entry into the civil services to landing up at the Green Park flat.

Believe me readers, right from CS upto the Green Park flat, living has been a painful transition from the fizzy excitement of youth to the seething stillness of midlife. But this journey with you through the first half returned the excitement to the stillness, life to living, and ultimately delivered 'I' to myself. Ruchi's prognosis that writing will fulfil me stands realized.

Now, I am caught up in an exciting impatience to take you through the next leg. And believe me, this later part is also full of exciting fun, romance, thoughts and perspectives on life; a slice of life with a different flavour. I sincerely thank you for travelling with me thus far and request you to wish me the karma to travel the second half.

Mukul Kumar
January 2016.

Acknowledgements

First and foremost, I would like to thank Lord Shiva who inspired this work. He is the sole one beyond the faith–doubt dichotomy, whom I have always found standing by my side, hand-holding me like a toddler through his writing journey.

Then Rakhi, my wife. She is the one who showed me the practical path to my passion through the maze of living. Avantika, my lovely daughter, is, along with my wife, the first audience to my story, sharpening my sight for the reader's perspective. My father, my eternal companion, was the first one to read the entire manuscript and made me believe that I had done it, besides rendering critical suggestions. My mother, of course, typically kept wishing her son his world and believing that her son is equal to any task. Manisha has been the one behind the scenes to afford me an ideal setting to ease out the rigours of the journey. Khushi Ram has done a wonderful job with regard to typing and organizing the manuscript.

Writing a book and making it reach the readers are separate legs of the journey. I express my sincere thanks to Kapish Mehra for believing in me. The team at Rupa Publications have done a great job with editing and packaging the book. Payel Roy Chowdhury, my friend, has been a constant support during the second leg of the journey with her valuable tips. Dr Avinash Unnithan and Prince Pande have also provided great support.

www.ingramcontent.com/pod-product-compliance
Lightning Source LLC
LaVergne TN
LVHW091051080826
845145LV00002B/709

* 9 7 8 8 1 2 9 1 3 8 5 2 1 *